P9-DFJ-216

UNDER PRESSURE

Also by Alex Morgan:

THE KICKS SERIES

SAVING THE TEAM

SABOTAGE SEASON

WIN OR LOSE

HAT TRICK

SHAKEN UP

SETTLE THE SCORE

BREAKAWAY: BEYOND THE GOAL

ALEX MORGAN

Simon & Schuster Books for Young Readers
New York London Toronto Sydney New Delhi

SIMON & SCHUSTER BOOKS FOR YOUNG READERS
An imprint of Simon & Schuster Children's Publishing Division
1230 Avenue of the Americas, New York, New York 10020

Book design by Krista Vossen
The text for this book was set in Berling.
Manufactured in the United States of America
0417 FFG
First Edition
2 4 6 8 10 9 7 5 3 1
CIP data for this book is available from the Library of Congress.
ISBN 978-1-4814-8150-2 (hardcover)
ISBN 978-1-4814-8152-6 (eBook)

CHAPTER ONE

My cleats were a blur as I raced across the soccer field, keeping the ball close to me. I darted quickly around the other players.

Was it my speed that got everyone's attention? Or my control of the ball? Nope.

"Devin, you haven't stopped smiling since you stepped onto the field," Jessi remarked, panting slightly as she ran alongside me.

My grin got even bigger. I was back on my home turf, surrounded by my best friends. How could I not smile? I was one of the Kicks again, and we were all together at our first practice of the spring season!

I used to live in Connecticut, where I could compete in soccer only during the spring and summer months. Here in California I could play all year long. When the school soccer season had ended in the fall, I'd been going into some serious soccer withdrawal. Jessi had suggested we try out for the winter league, and I had jumped at the chance.

The winter soccer season had ended a few weeks ago, and even though I'd been a member of the champion team, the Griffons, I had been eagerly waiting for the spring soccer season to start. Now that it had, I was with my friends, playing on the Kentville Middle School Kangaroos (otherwise known as the Kicks) again. As a Griffon I'd had to compete against some of my very best friends. That had been tough. But now we were all on the same side once more. Together we would be unstoppable!

An image of the Kicks sweeping the spring season and being crowned champions flashed through my mind. I pictured the crowd, dressed in the Kicks' colors of blue and white, chanting our team's name. I had just scored the winning goal. My teammates hoisted me up on their shoulders, cheering as we celebrated. I guess I got a little too caught up in my fantasy, because I was taken totally by surprise when I felt something push against the front of my shoulder, throwing me off balance. I fought to regain my equilibrium, but it was too late. I had lost control of the ball.

I saw a girl running away with it, her curly brown hair bouncing on her shoulders as she raced down the field.

"Way to fight for the ball, Hailey," I heard Coach Flores shout approvingly. "Perfect use of your body to win the ball!"

Whenever Coach Flores yelled, she still sounded nice, no matter what she was saying. Coach Darby from the

Griffons was always barking at us, whether she was praising or correcting. She was tough, and I learned a lot from her. Yet I couldn't be happier to be back with Coach Flores—except that I wanted her compliments directed at me! (Okay, I'll admit it, I'm competitive.)

Hailey charged down the field with the stolen ball. She passed it to Grace, who was the co-captain of the Kicks with me. Grace sent the ball flying over the grassy field, over the goalie's head, and into the net. Everyone clapped and cheered.

"Go, new girl!" Maya, one of the eighth-grade players, yelled. Hailey was a new student at Kentville Middle School and new to the Kicks, too. She was a seventh grader, like me and my best friends on the team—Jessi, Zoe, Emma, and Frida.

"Her name is Hailey," Jessi called to Maya, her hands on her hips. "And something tells me you won't forget it."

As we switched sides to continue our practice game, Jessi gave me a knowing grin. "She's going to give you a run for your money, Devin," she teased.

"That's why I encouraged Hailey to join," I replied. "I want the Kicks to be the best they can be!"

Yet even as I said this to Jessi, I felt a pang of jealousy rise up inside me. My friends knew I was competitive too. They also knew that I ate, slept, and breathed soccer. I did want our entire team to be the strongest it could be, yet part of me wanted to be the strongest of the strong. Was that so terrible?

The ball was in play, so I didn't have time to dwell on Hailey or anything else. The other team in our practice game had control of the ball. Brianna raced toward our goal, her blond hair flying behind her. Frida, a defender, stood between Brianna and the goal. While Brianna drew closer, Frida stood gazing up at the sky, completely oblivious to what was happening.

Giselle, the other defender closest to Frida, yelled in frustration. "Frida! Look alive!"

At the sound of her name, Frida turned her head from the clouds back to the field. It was too late. Brianna was in striking distance. Giselle rushed in to descend on her, but Brianna quickly took her shot. Our team's goalie, Emma, dove to catch the ball, but she missed. It hit the back of the net, hard.

Jessi looked at me, one eyebrow arched questioningly. "Frida's head was totally somewhere else," she said. "Maybe back on the movie set?"

Frida was a good soccer player and an even better actor. She had recently had a starring role in the TV movie *Mall Mania* with teen pop star Brady McCoy. Impressive, right? When I'd lived in Connecticut, I hadn't known anybody who was a TV star. It was just one of the many ways life was different in California, like mild winters and having to always be careful to conserve water. An actor friend was by far the most glamorous thing about living in Cali, although I enjoyed being able to wear flip-flops pretty much year round too.

I shrugged. We all had our bad moments on the soccer field. Frida being inattentive at a practice wasn't the end of the world.

"She'll shake it off," I said. "It's only the first practice of the season. Maybe she's just rusty because she didn't play in winter league, like the rest of us."

But Frida didn't shake it off. After our scrimmage Coach Flores had us work on a simple passing and receiving drill. When Emma tried to pass the ball to her, Frida was looking up at the sky again.

"Oops, Frida!" Emma said in that cheerful way she had. "Maybe I overshot that."

Jessi gave me a pointed look. We all knew Emma had been on target. Frida hadn't been paying attention again.

When Frida passed the ball to Zoe, it went far and wide. It was nowhere near Zoe. Actually, it was nowhere near anyone else, either. Frida, who was usually very dramatic and expressive, was very quiet. After each mistake she made, she looked at the ground or up at the sky. She didn't react at all. Maybe Jessi was right and something was up with Frida.

Frida continued blundering her way through practice. After Coach blew the final whistle, Jessi, Zoe, Emma, and I ran up to her.

"Is everything okay, Frida?" Emma asked. She put a hand on Frida's shoulder, and I noticed that Emma seemed even taller than usual. She must have had a growth spurt over the winter.

Zoe peered out from underneath her strawberry-blond bangs. "Yeah, is anything wrong?"

In the beginning of the school year, Frida hadn't wanted to play soccer, but her mom had made her. After we gave Frida the idea to imagine she was playing a different character in each game, Frida began to love soccer as much as the rest of us. She pretended to be everything from a fairy princess to a military commander to a space alien. Not only did it help Frida play better, but it made the games much more fun for the rest of us. I'll never forget the looks on the opposing team's faces when she yelled at them, "Surrender, earthlings!" We all still laughed about that.

But today Frida wasn't laughing. She didn't seem angry. Or upset. She was just . . . quiet. Which was really weird for Frida.

"Nothing's wrong," Frida said in a quiet, mousy voice that was very un-Frida-like. She shrugged. "It's nothing."

We all exchanged worried glances as Frida turned away from us and jogged back toward the locker rooms.

Emma's brown eyes got big with concern. "What's up with Frida?"

Zoe frowned. "Do you think she doesn't want to play anymore now that she's a famous actor?"

I hadn't thought about that. Frida had chosen acting over playing in the winter league. If it had been me, I would never have given up soccer for anything, even to star in a movie. It just went to show that even though we were all Kicks, we were all different. Zoe loved fashion and had dreams of being a designer one day, but she was just as competitive as I was when it came to soccer. She was one of the first friends I'd made after I'd moved here from Connecticut, but during the winter season she'd been on a different team, the Gators. When the Gators had faced off against the Griffons for the championship, it had put a lot of stress on our friendship. We worked through it, though. And now, thankfully, we were better friends than ever.

With the Kicks finally back together, the thought that Frida might quit was stressing me out. But I didn't want to start panicking yet.

"Are we still on for your house this Saturday, Jessi?" I asked.

Jessi nodded. "You bet! My mom is even letting me pick out total junk food snacks. I know she feels guilty about making me give up my bedroom, so I can ask her for just about anything right now and she says yes."

"That'll probably stop once your new baby brother or sister comes around," Zoe said.

Jessi's eyes narrowed. "What did I tell you? Do not say the *B* word, please. I have four more months of peace, and I want to enjoy them."

Emma laughed. "Well, at least we know what's bugging you, Jessi. Too bad we don't know what's up with Frida."

"It's pretty obvious that Frida doesn't want to talk about whatever is bothering her now," I said. "Maybe whatever it is will have blown over by Saturday. If not, we'll talk to her then and figure out what's going on."

"And how we can help her," Zoe added.

That was exactly what I loved about my Kicks friends. We definitely had each other's backs, both on and off the soccer field. I was so psyched to be back, and couldn't wait for the season to begin.

Grace started clapping her hands loudly. "Great first practice, everyone. This is going to be an amazing season. Let's sound off!"

All of the remaining Kicks quickly formed a circle.

"I don't know but I've been told!" Grace began.

"I don't know but I've been told!" we repeated.

"This year the Kicks will grab the gold!" she shouted.

"This year the Kicks will grab the gold!"

"No one can beat us on the field!"

"No one can beat us on the field!"

"And when we play, we never yield!"

"And when we play, we never yield!"

"Sound off!

"One, two!"

"Sound off!"

"Three, four!"

Then we all cheered together. "Sound off. One, two, three, four—sound off!"

CHAPTER TWO

Saturday morning Mom dropped me off at Jessi's house.

"What time should I pick you up?" she asked as I took off my seat belt.

"I'm not sure. This might take a while," I replied. "Mrs. Dukes is making us lunch."

"Text me when you're done," Mom said. "And not too much soda, Devin!"

"I won't!" I promised as I jogged to the door. But I knew there would be at least one root beer in my future.

When I rang the doorbell, Jessi answered me from inside. "Come on up!"

I pushed open the door and ran upstairs. Jessi's bedroom door was wide open. I walked in, and my jaw dropped.

"Oh, wow," I said. "Was there an earthquake in here?"

Jessi, Emma, and Zoe were standing in the room, surrounded on all sides by cardboard boxes. Piles of clothes were mounded on Jessi's bed. Her empty dresser drawers were stacked on the floor.

"Finally, you're here!" Jessi cried. "Can you please move that box? We're sort of trapped."

She pointed to a box, and I picked it up. It was so heavy, I had to drag it across the floor. "What's in here?" I asked. "A bunch of rocks?"

"Those are my scrapbooks," Jessi explained. "I had to do something in the days before Instagram."

"You should see her trophy collection," Zoe said. "And her sneaker collection. And her DVD collection."

Emma picked one of the DVDs out of the box. "Oh, *The Sunshine Puppies*! I loved them."

"So, you've saved everything you've ever had since you were a baby?" I guessed.

"No *B* word!" Jessi snapped. "That . . . you know . . . is the reason I have to leave my beautiful room in the first place."

"Why exactly do you have to move, again?" I asked.

"So the you-know-what can have a room next to Mom and Dad," Jessi replied. "There are only two bedrooms up here. I'm moving to the room downstairs that used to be Dad's office."

"Unless his office is like Doctor Who's TARDIS, you're going to be in trouble," Emma said, and Zoe laughed.

"Can you translate for those of us who don't speak nerd?" I teased.

"The TARDIS is bigger on the inside," Emma explained. "And Jessi's new room, right now, appears to be very small."

"I'll show you," Jessi said.

We followed her downstairs and walked past the kitchen. Jessi's dad was doing dishes, and her mom was looking at a take-out menu.

"Hey, girls!" Mrs. Dukes greeted us. "Is Frida coming? I'm going to order the pizza soon and want to make sure to get enough."

"Extra pepperoni, please," Jessi said. "And chicken wings. And yes, Frida's supposed to be coming."

Mrs. Dukes rubbed her belly, where Jessi's baby brother or sister was growing. "This one loves pepperoni. Go figure," she said. "Extra pepperoni it is!"

"See? You and your new sibling have something in common already," Mr. Dukes said encouragingly, but Jessi just rolled her eyes.

"Come on," she told us. "Let me show you my new prison."

She led us to a small room off the dining room, and we all stepped inside.

"Definitely not bigger on the inside," Emma said.

"Seriously, Jessi, how are you going to fit everything in here?" Zoe asked. "I don't even see a closet."

"Mom says I have to purge," Jessi answered. "But what am I supposed to give up?"

"How about *The Sunshine Puppies* boxed set?" I suggested.

"Those are part of my childhood!" Jessi argued. "And besides, the b—" She caught herself in time. "The new member of the family might want to watch them."

Emma put an arm around her. "Oh, that's sweet, Jessi. You do have a soft spot for the *B* word after all!"

Jessi sighed. "I guess. I'm just bummed that things are changing, though," she said. She motioned around the room. "How am I supposed to live in here? Upstairs I have a view of the beautiful blue sky. Down here I have a view of the recycling cans!"

Zoe walked to the window. "Yeah, that is a bummer."

"It won't be so bad," I said. "At least you and the . . . At least you won't have to share a room with anyone. Maisie and I had to share before we moved out here. That was such a pain!"

"And we can make this room totes adorbs!" Emma said. "You'll see. But first we should go back to your room and finish packing."

"And purging," Zoe added. "It'll be like that show *Tiny Living,* where people get rid of all their stuff and move into insanely small houses. We'll make a game of it."

"Oh boy. That sounds like so much fun," Jessi said in a flat voice.

I lightly punched her in the arm. "Come on, let's give it a try."

Once we were back upstairs, Zoe picked up a plaid shirt from Jessi's bed.

"When was the last time you wore this?" she asked.

Jessi frowned. "Um, I don't know. Maybe last year?"

"Toss!" Zoe cried, throwing the shirt onto the floor. "That goes in the giveaway pile. So does anything else you haven't worn in the past six months."

Jessi looked horrified. "Even my lucky sweater? It doesn't fit me anymore, but I still keep it."

"Yes!" Zoe said firmly.

"Don't be cruel, Zoe," Emma said. "Let the girl keep her lucky sweater."

Zoe's eyes narrowed. "We'll see."

It took us almost an hour to go through Jessi's clothes. Zoe held them up one by one and helped Jessi decide whether to keep them or not. Emma bagged up the give-away stuff, and I folded the "keep clothes" and boxed them. Zoe looked completely satisfied when we had finished.

"Excellent!" she said, her blue eyes gleaming. "Now let's start on those sneakers."

"Nobody is touching my sneakers!" Jessi protested, and before Zoe could argue, Jessi's mom called up to us.

"Pizza's here!" she yelled. "And so is Frida!"

We raced downstairs. Jessi's dad was carrying three pizza boxes into the kitchen, and Frida stood in the doorway.

"Sorry I'm late!" she apologized. Her cheeks were flushed, and tendrils of her wavy, auburn hair were coming loose from her ponytail. "I was at some dumb audition and they made me wait forever and it was all for nothing anyway."

"So you didn't get the part?" I asked.

"No," Frida said, looking down at her sandals. Then her voice became a mumble. "But why would I, anyway?"

Jessi and I looked at each other. We were both starting to figure out why Frida had been in such a weird mood. Jessi put an arm around her. "Come on. Let's go eat some pizza," she said.

We went into the kitchen and filled our plates with salad, pizza, and chicken wings. Then the five of us went outside to eat at the patio table.

Frida had put on her plate only some salad and one lonely chicken wing. She picked at her food with a fork while the rest of us started gobbling pizza.

"All that purging made me hungry!" Emma remarked.

"Well, it made me lose my appetite, but luckily, I've got it back," Jessi said, taking a bite of her pepperoni slice.

Zoe turned to Frida. "Things will go faster now that you're here," she said. "Sorry about your audition."

Frida didn't say anything. I got the idea that maybe her auditions hadn't gone well, and that's why she had been in a bad mood lately.

"Frida, we can tell something's been upsetting you," I said. "Do you feel like talking about it?"

Frida looked at each of us, one by one, as if deciding if she could do it. "It's not easy," she said finally.

"Frida, we are your friends till the end," Emma said. "If you can't talk to us, who can you talk to?"

Frida nodded. "You're right," she said. Then she took a deep breath and began. "After *Mall Mania* came out, I was sure I was going to have casting directors knocking down my door, looking to hire me. But I haven't booked a single job since then! I was, like, so close to being famous, and now I'm back to being a nobody!"

Zoe raised an eyebrow. "You mean like the rest of us?"

"Of course that's not what I mean," Frida replied. "You wouldn't understand. It's an actor thing. You're only as good as your next job. But there is no job for me. I'm a has-been at thirteen!"

"No way!" I cried. "Frida, you're just beginning. Nobody becomes famous overnight."

"Of course they do," she said. "Look at James Dean. Or Kim Kardashian."

Zoe rolled her eyes. "I'd rather not."

"I'm just saying, I had my fifteen minutes of fame, and I could have turned it into an hour, or a week, or a decade," Frida said, her voice rising. "Instead I'm sliding backward into oblivion!"

"Oblivion's not so bad," Jessi said, holding up her slice. "We have good pizza here."

Frida shook her head. "I knew you guys wouldn't understand."

I felt so bad. This conversation wasn't going the way it was supposed to.

"We'll try to understand, Frida, promise," I said. "We'll help you get through this. Maybe you're just off your game. It happens to the best of us."

Frida sighed. "Maybe."

I frowned. The gears in my mind started spinning like they always do when one of my friends has a problem. We would have to find some way to help Frida. I hated seeing her so unhappy. And besides—we needed her head in the game when she played for the Kicks!

CHAPTER THREE

We helped Jessi with her bedroom for the rest of the afternoon. By the time we finished, we had four bags and three boxes of stuff to give away. We moved the rest down to Jessi's new room.

"Stage two will be decorating," Zoe said. "We'll make this your dream room, I promise."

Jessi looked around at the boxes and bags, frowning. "Until then I guess I'm sleeping on the couch," she said. "My bed doesn't even fit in here!"

"Make sure you get plenty of sleep before the pep rally on Monday," I told her, and Jessi shook her head.

"And Devin takes it back to soccer, as always!" she teased.

As we'd been finishing, I had texted my mom to pick me up. Now my cell phone dinged, and I looked to see that she was outside.

"Gotta go," I said. "See you Monday!"

When I got to the car, I saw Maisie in the backseat. She was eight years old and, for some reason, could bug me more than any other person on earth. I was relieved to see she was playing some kind of game on her tablet involving ladybugs. That meant she'd be quiet on the ride home.

"How did it go?" Mom asked.

"We got a lot done," I reported as I strapped on my seat belt. "I feel sorry for Jessi, though. She's got to totally rearrange her whole life for her new brother or sister."

I emphasized "sister" with a glance back at Maisie.

Mom shook her head. "One day you'll be so grateful that you have a sister, Devin. Trust me. I don't know what I'd do without Aunt Amy, and she's six years younger than I am. She used to drive me crazy too."

This was something I hadn't thought about before. "Like how?"

"Like, she was always taking my stuff without asking, and whenever we went on a car trip, she sang along to the radio with the loudest voice in the universe," Mom said.

I nodded. "That would drive me crazy."

"But now she's one of the most important people in my life," Mom said, and she quickly started to tear up a little. "I miss her so much, you know?"

"I miss her too," I said. "And Grandma and Grandpa."

Mom's family had all lived pretty close to us when we'd lived in Connecticut. But my grandparents on my dad's side lived in Florida. His brothers, Uncle Matt and Uncle Drew, lived far away too. One lived in Chicago, I think, and the other one was in Cleveland or something. So we hardly ever saw them.

My mom and I were both quiet during the rest of the drive. I couldn't stop thinking about Grandma and Grandpa, how Grandma always smelled like peppermints when I hugged her, and how Grandpa's big laugh seemed to fill the room whenever I told him a silly joke when I was a little kid.

So it was pretty awesome when I walked into the house and found Dad at the kitchen table on his laptop.

"Here she is!" he was saying to the screen. "You can tell her the good news yourself."

"Who is it?" I asked, and Dad got up so I could take his place in the chair. There on the screen was Grandma! Her brown hair was cut cute and short, but I knew from pictures that she used to wear it long, just like me.

"Noodles!" Grandma cried, using her nickname for me.

"Hey, Grandma," I said. "What's the good news?"

"Grandpa and I just bought our plane tickets!" she said. "We're coming out to see you."

By now Maisie was trying to climb onto the chair with me. "I'm here too, Grandma! It's Maisie!"

"Maisie, chill!" I said. "I'll make room for you, but you have to stop climbing all over me."

Grandma shook her head. "Just like your mother and your aunt Amy, you two."

"That's what Mom just told me," I said. "So when are you coming?"

Grandma's eyes twinkled. "That's the best part, Noodles!

We'll be there in time to see your first Kicks game of the season. Isn't that exciting?"

"That is awesome!" I said. I loved the idea of Grandma and Grandpa cheering me in the stands. But then it hit me.

"Um, can you do me a favor and maybe not call me Noodles when you're here?" I asked.

Grandma looked a little sad. "Oh, I understand. You're not a little girl anymore, are you?"

"Noodles! Noodles!" Maisie chanted.

I rolled my eyes. "Was Aunt Amy really this bad?"

"Your mother thought so," Grandma said. "But Maisie's not being bad. She's just full of energy. Right, Maisie?"

"Noodles!" Maisie replied.

Mom tapped my shoulder. "Can I please talk to Grandma?"

"Sure," I told her. "Bye, Grandma. See you soon!"

"Good-bye, my grown-up Devin. Good-bye, Maisie!" she said.

Maisie and I got up from the chair, and Dad walked up to me.

"Devin, can you wash your hands and help me make dinner?" he asked.

"Sure," I said. "What are we having?"

"Whole wheat spaghetti with broccoli," he replied.

"Noodles!" Maisie cheered, and I groaned.

I couldn't wait to see Grandma, but I hoped she would leave my nickname back in Connecticut!

CHAPTER FOUR

On Monday morning I stood in front of the full-length mirror in my room, my cell phone in my hand. I was wearing my blue-and-white Kicks jersey, denim capris, and flip-flops—one white and one blue. My long, brown hair was pulled back into a ponytail with one of the blue-and-white sparkly scrunchies that Coach Flores had given to all the Kicks to wear today.

I smiled and snapped a selfie. I texted the pic to Kara, my best friend in Connecticut, with the message, *Pep rally 2day!*

Since there was a three-hour time difference between California and Connecticut, I didn't know when she'd get a chance to reply, but it was something we did just about every day. When I'd woken up this morning, there'd been a text from Kara with a picture. She was wearing a pair of jeans, a sweatshirt with tiny hearts all over it, and boots.

She wore her hair in a messy bun on the top of her head. She was making an exaggerated sad face, her lips pulled down into an oversize frown. *Overslept!*

I'd laughed out loud when I'd seen it. Kara had a hard time waking up every morning. She was always barely making it to the bus on time, which drove her mom crazy. Yet she still found the time to text me!

Sitting in class that morning was tough. I was a good student, and it was usually easy for me to concentrate, but I found myself tapping my foot impatiently a few times. I was just too excited for the pep rally that afternoon. It was being held to kick off the beginning of the spring soccer season. Both the boys' and girls' teams would be celebrated today.

When Jessi, Zoe, Emma, Frida, and I finally walked into the gym that afternoon with the rest of our team, I felt myself getting even more pumped up. A bunch of blue and white balloons floated above the podium on the gym floor. And a big banner hung from the basketball backboard. It had a picture of a kangaroo on it kicking a soccer ball, and the words, "Go, Kangaroos!" It looked like it had been recycled from the pep rally that had been held for us last fall when we'd made it to the championships. It's hard to describe the feeling of having all your classmates and teachers come out to support you. But I can tell you this: It's pretty awesome!

"Wow!" Emma said, her eyes wide. "I'll never get used

to this. It looks like the entire school is here to cheer us on again."

"The entire school *is* here. It's a school-wide assembly," Zoe said as we watched sixth graders, seventh graders, and eighth graders fill the bleachers. Since Zoe's pixie hairstyle was too short for a ponytail, she wore her blue-and-white Kicks scrunchie on her wrist.

"An adoring crowd. I love it!" Frida said, finally sounding more like herself.

"It's good to see you feeling better," Jessi remarked. "See, I told you it wasn't so bad being part of the oblivion."

Frida shook her head. "I tried to explain it to you, but that is a fate worse than death, Jessi," she said in her usual over-the-top way. "No, what's got me feeling better is that my mom texted right before the pep rally. I have an audition after school today. And I think it's going to go really well."

"You'll do great, Frida. After all, you're the most talented actor I know," Emma said, upbeat and positive like always.

"I'm also the only actor you know," Frida reminded her, and we all laughed.

As we lined up next to Coach Flores, I saw the boys' team lining up too. They stood next to their coach, Coach Valentine. Our friends Steven and Cody were there, and Steven gave me a wave and a smile. I waved back, and I heard Jessi yelling, "Cody!" He looked up and grinned.

"Jessi!" he yelled back.

Jessi and I liked hanging out with them. To be clear, I liked hanging out with Steven, and Jessi liked hanging out with Cody, and we all liked hanging out together. I wasn't allowed to date yet, but if I could have, Steven would have been a contender. He was supercute and very nice, and he loved soccer just as much as I did.

Before I could think more about how cute Steven's smile was, a drumbeat echoed through the gymnasium. The marching band paraded into the gym, playing an upbeat tune. The cheerleaders, dressed in blue and white, waved their pom-poms from the sidelines and danced.

When the song was over and the applause had finished, Principal Gallegos got in front of the crowd, holding a microphone. He always wore a suit. Today he wore it with a white shirt and blue tie—school and Kicks colors. This pep rally was just as impressive as the one they'd held before the state championship! I got the feeling that the school was expecting big things from us this season.

"Good afternoon!" Principal Gallegos's loud voice boomed out across the gymnasium. He didn't even need a microphone. "We're here to start off the spring soccer season with some Kentville spirit! Our boys' team will be a force to be reckoned with. Let's give it up for Coach Valentine and the Kangaroos!"

"Coach! Coach! Coach!" the boys chanted as Coach Valentine waved to the crowd. His team loved him, but he was tough. When he had subbed for Coach Flores last season, my arms had ached from all the push-ups he'd made us do. My legs hadn't felt much better from all the laps we'd had to run either.

After Principal Gallegos introduced the captains of the boys' team, the cheerleaders did a dance routine, complete with jumps, flips, and lifts, to a high-energy pop song. The kids in the bleachers went crazy, cheering and stomping. The sound echoed through the gym.

I guess I'm not the only one pumped up today! I thought. Even if you didn't like soccer (although that was hard for me to imagine!), most kids liked being at a pep rally better than sitting in math class.

"Now," the principal said after the applause had finally quieted down, "I'd like to introduce our girls' Kangaroos soccer team, or as we like to call them, the Kicks. They are returning to the field this season after playing in the state championship tournament. To ensure that they have everything they need to succeed this spring, Sally Lane of Lane's Sporting Goods will be donating even more new equipment to help them reach their goals. Ms. Lane, please stand up."

A tall, blond woman rose from her seat in the first row of the bleachers.

"Let's give Ms. Lane a round of applause!" Principal Gallegos said. Everyone clapped enthusiastically, and Ms. Lane smiled.

"This is crazy!" Jessi had to shout above all the noise. "Just think of what we started with last season. Soon our field will be better than the boys'!"

When I had first joined the Kicks, the team had been practicing on a shabby field with two bright orange trash cans for the goalposts. It was totally lame, and it had been hard not to get upset about it, especially since the boys' team had a much nicer field with top-notch equipment. After the Kicks had started winning, Sally Lane had donated real goalposts. To think she was going to donate even more equipment made me really happy. I wasn't the only one. Coach Flores had the biggest smile I had ever seen on her face. Grace and Anjali high-fived, Sarah and Anna hugged each other, and the rest of the team was screaming their heads off in excitement and jumping up and down.

"Now, this doesn't come without a price," Principal Gallegos said. "We are hoping that the Kicks will add the state championship trophy to the Kentville Middle School's trophy case."

State championship? Principal Gallegos sure wanted us to aim high. I was in total agreement with him. I wanted to be a part of bringing that honor to Kentville.

"Let's meet the Kicks soccer team captains who will carry us to victory," Principal Gallegos continued. "Grace Kirkland and Devin Burke, come forward."

As Grace and I stood next to Principal Gallegos, the cheers and applause continued. I could hear hoots and hollers coming from the stands. The entire school had been rooting for us when we'd gone to the state championships. In fact, the entire town had shown their support.

It had been a really big deal. I couldn't help but notice that we got even more cheers than the boys' captains had.

At first I felt pretty great, standing up there and getting all that applause. But then I began to feel the pressure. All those faces looking at us, expecting us to do well. Not just do well but be the best in the state! Principal Gallegos and Ms. Lane were beaming at us as they clapped. Principal Gallegos had basically said we owed it to Ms. Lane to win the state championships. When we'd lost the last time, I had taken it hard. We had tried our best and given it our all. Everyone had been amazed at how far we had come. But back then no one had expected anything from the Kicks. Before I had joined the team, they had won only one game the year before. And that was because the other team had forfeited! Now everyone was talking about winning state.

Blue and white confetti started to fall around me and Grace. The band began playing again. As I stood there, the butterflies in my stomach began banging their own drums in time to the music. Could the Kicks repeat the magic we'd had in the fall? And if we didn't, would we let everyone down?

CHAPTER FIVE

At lunch the next day Jessi, Emma, Zoe, Frida, and I all sat together at the same table. It was another reason why I was excited that we were all back on the Kicks. During the winter Frida had been away making her TV movie. Emma, who hadn't made a winter league team, had joined the school's environmental club, the Tree Huggers, and she would eat lunch with them some days. Jessi and I had been on the Griffons, but Zoe and some of the other Kicks, like my co-captain, Grace, had been on the Gators. The Gators had eaten lunch together in order to strategize. It had been awkward, to say the least.

But that was behind us. Now I could focus on playing soccer (and eating lunch!) with my best friends again.

As Jessi unpacked her lunch from her bag, I heard her singing softly under her breath.

"You are my sunshine—woof, woof—my only

sunshine—woof, woof. You make my tail wag—woof, woof—when skies are gray," she sang.

Emma giggled and pointed at Jessi. Zoe and Frida looked at Jessi and started cracking up.

"Jessi, were you watching *The Sunshine Puppies*?" I asked teasingly.

"It makes her tail wag!" Emma laughed.

"Woof, woof!" Zoe and Frida barked at the same time, which had us all hysterically laughing, even Jessi.

"I couldn't help it," Jessi admitted once we had all calmed down. "After you guys left on Saturday, I was feeling really sorry for myself. And the DVD was just sitting there, staring at me."

"Hypnotizing you," Frida joked. Then she put on a monotone voice. "You are getting sleepy. You must watch me."

"So I just popped it in," Jessi continued, ignoring Frida. "And you know what? It made me feel better. I'm not gonna lie."

I got that. Sometimes when Maisie was watching her silly kids' shows, I would sit on the couch and pretend to be busy on my phone, but I would secretly be watching too. I wasn't going to admit that to everyone, though.

"It's okay, Jessi," I said instead. "It's good practice to get used to those shows again for when the baby comes."

As soon as the word "baby" came out of my mouth, I realized the mistake I had made. Jessi's eyes narrowed as she looked at me.

"Oops, sorry, I meant 'the *B* word'!" I said. "Don't be

mad, Jessi. After all, you are my sunshine!"

We all laughed so loudly that kids sitting at the tables around us got quiet and stared at us.

"I'm not ashamed," Jessi called out to them. "I love *The Sunshine Puppies*!"

That did it. Emma spurted a mouthful of water onto the table, she was laughing so hard, which of course just set us off even further.

After we finally calmed down again and cleaned up the water, the talk turned to the pep rally the day before.

"Now I know what you must have felt like on the red carpet for your movie premiere, Frida," Emma said, and beamed. "It was like we were rock stars or something."

Jessi nodded in agreement. "So many kids were coming up to me afterward to wish me good luck for the season. Even Trey Bishop!"

We all gasped at that. The Kicks had performed a lot better than the boys' team last fall. Some of the boys, like Steven and Cody, had been disappointed that they hadn't made it further but had been happy for us. Trey, an eighth grader, had been nasty to the Kicks, especially me. But the other eighth graders on the Kicks had stuck up for me, and Trey had backed down.

"What happened to him?" I wondered.

"Was he being sarcastic?" Zoe asked.

Jessi shrugged. "He seemed real, but we'll see. If the Kicks go further than the boys again, that will be the real test."

"Frida!" Emma said suddenly, like she had just

remembered something. "You need to tell us about your audition. What was it for? How did it go?"

Frida smiled. "I'm pretty sure I nailed it. It was for a fruit snack commercial. They seemed to really like me."

"I'm sure you got it, Frida," Emma said enthusiastically. "You're the best!"

"If I could land something, anything, at this point, it would give my confidence a big boost," Frida shared. "Otherwise I have to rethink my entire existence on this planet!"

Jessi and I exchanged smiles. It was good to see Frida back to being her old, dramatic self.

I started munching on the sandwich my mom had made for me: turkey with cucumber and hummus on a whole wheat pita, with some carrot sticks and a yogurt on the side. Sometimes I complained about my mom being so strict about soda, candy, and cookies, but really I was glad. As an athlete, it was important for me to eat healthfully. Besides, I still got to have treats, like at Jessi's house the other day. My friends and I also loved going out, especially after games and practices, for burritos, frozen yogurt, and other fun foods.

"How far have you gotten in the reading assignment?" Jessi asked me. We were in the same English class together.

Before I could answer her, Frida gave a strangled cry. I looked up, alarmed. We all knew Frida liked to be dramatic, but this sounded different from anything I had ever heard from her.

"Are you okay?" I asked. Frida was staring at her phone. All the color had drained from her face.

"I didn't get the part," she said softly and slowly at first. Then she yelled, "I didn't get it!"

Her shock and hurt were evident. This wasn't Frida acting. She was really, really upset.

Emma got up and ran around the table to put her arms around Frida. "It's okay," she said soothingly. "You'll get the next one."

Frida pushed Emma away. "You don't understand!" she wailed. "Nobody wants me. I've tried and tried. If I can't land a part right after starring in *Mall Mania,* it's over. Over!"

Tears began streaming down Frida's face. She stood up, grabbed her things, and ran out of the cafeteria before we could say anything else.

"Oh no! Poor Frida!" Emma cried. She looked almost as upset as Frida had been.

"Emma and I are done eating, so we'll go after her," Zoe said. She stood up and began hurriedly packing up her stuff as Emma did the same. "We'll bring her back."

They hurried out of the cafeteria. I put down my sandwich. Seeing Frida so upset had made me lose my appetite.

Jessi, on the other hand, continued to eat her wrap. "I don't understand," she said between bites, "why anyone would want to be in show business. It's so competitive."

I thought about that. "I guess, but soccer is too. After all, we had to try out for the winter league. Not everyone made it."

Jessi nodded. "That's true. I guess if you really want something, and you don't get it, it's going to hurt, no matter what it is."

Emma and Zoe returned to the table, but Frida wasn't with them.

"Frida went to the nurse's office," Zoe explained. "She didn't want to talk to us. She just wants to go home."

"She looked so upset, and she couldn't stop crying," Emma said. She frowned. "I hate seeing her like that. Frida is usually so confident."

"I'm worried about her too," I added. "The pressure is really getting to her!"

"I wish there was something we could say to make her feel better." Jessi shook her head sadly. "But everything we say seems to be the wrong thing and just makes her more upset."

"There must be some way to help her," Zoe pleaded. "There's got to be something we can do."

Emma sighed. "It's too bad we don't know any other actors who have been through rejection. If Frida had someone she could talk to about this, someone who has been through the same thing and could understand how she is feeling, it might help."

"Hmmmm." Jessi tapped her finger on her chin. She looked lost in thought. "Emma, that gave me an idea. I'll have to look into it some more. But it might be exactly what Frida needs to get over this!"

CHAPTER SIX

Frida was quiet for the next two days. She seemed embarrassed about freaking out during lunch, and we all got the vibe that she didn't want to talk about it—so we didn't.

I was glad to see her at Thursday's Kicks practice, though. We were having a scrimmage against the Pinewood Panthers, the team from the fancy private school a few towns away. They'd never had to train in a field with garbage can goalposts, and their players were all fiercely competitive.

We all got into our Kicks uniforms in the school locker room and then walked to the Kicks field for the scrimmage.

"Gather round!" Coach Flores said. We all ran to form a circle around her. "After this season is over, Sally Lane has agreed to pay for resodding our entire field!"

The Kicks cheered.

"No more kicking up dust when we play," Jessi said next to me.

"Or tripping over rocks," Emma added.

"That Sally Lane is like a soccer genie or something," I said. "I can't wait to get on that field and play!"

"Let's warm up, team!" Coach Flores called out. "Twice around the field!"

I started jogging, and Jessi ran alongside me. As we finished our first lap, a gleaming white bus pulled up to the parking lot. The word "Panthers" was written in script in purple and gold along the side.

"Looks like the Panthers are here," Jessi said.

The bus parked, and as we watched the doors open, I literally gasped. A woman with spiky blond hair stepped off the bus. She wore purple sweatpants and a gold Panthers jersey, and had a whistle around her neck.

"Coach Darby!" Jessi and I said at the same time.

Our winter-season coach was now coaching the Panthers! I started to feel the butterflies in my stomach. Coach Darby was strict and tough, and demanded excellence from her players. Her fierce coaching, combined with the aggressive Panthers players, was going to be tough to beat.

Then the Panthers marched off the bus, like soldiers marching in the army. They were doing a version of our chant.

"I don't know but I've been told!

"Panthers are gonna get the gold.

"We can't be stopped, we can't be beat!

"Because we've all got magic feet!"

Coach Darby blew her whistle. "All right, girls, let's see

you warm up in unison!" she yelled, and the players started jogging around the field in single file.

I knew the girl at the very end of the line, the one with the long, black braids. Mirabelle had started out on the Kicks, and then transferred to Pinewood. We had started out as total enemies, but we had become friends when we'd ended up on the Griffons together in the winter league.

Jessi and I slowed down our jog to talk to her.

"Hey, Mirabelle," I said. "Coach Darby's with the Panthers? That must be interesting."

Mirabelle nodded. "It'll be interesting when we wipe the field with you losers," she said.

Jessi and I looked at each other.

"Seriously?" Jessi asked. "I understand that we're competing, but I thought we were cool."

"We're not cool," Mirabelle said. "I've got to get another scholarship next year, and I can't lose focus."

"You can stay focused and still be nice," I said.

"Maybe you can," Mirabelle replied. "Not me. Let's see how that works for you today."

Jessi and I shook our heads and jogged away.

"Wow, I really thought she had changed," I said.

"My dad always says that a leopard never changes its spots," Jessi replied. "Now I know what he means."

When we returned to our side of the field, Grace was getting the players into a circle.

"First lucky sock swap of the spring!" she called out.

Jessi and I joined the circle and sat down on the grass.

The Kicks had started the tradition in the fall, and it always raised our spirits before a game. We each took off one sock (Coach Flores let us wear socks with any pattern we wanted) and passed it to the teammate on our left. That way, on the field, none of us wore matching socks.

Jessi was sitting to my left, and she passed me a sock with rainbow polka dots on it. It looked pretty cool along with my other sock, neon pink with black zebra stripes. Ever since we'd been doing the sock swap, my mom had been on the lookout for fun socks I could wear.

When we'd finished swapping, we jumped up and each put a hand into the center of the circle.

"Goooooo, Kicks!" we cheered.

"Okay, girls!" Coach Flores said. "This is just a scrimmage, so don't get too stressed out. Just do your best, like I know you can. Zarine, you're starting on goal. Let's see Sarah, Anjali, Jade, and Frida on defense. Jessi, Taylor, Maya, you're my midfield. Devin, Hailey, Grace, I want you on forward."

I nodded, excited to be starting the game. I looked up into the stands. They had quickly filled with Kicks fans—parents, brothers and sisters, and Kentville students. I saw Mom and Dad with Maisie, and waved.

The Kicks starters jogged onto the field and took our positions. Grace faced off against one of the Panthers' forwards, the ref blew his whistle, and the game began.

The Panthers player got control of the ball and quickly sent a long pass lobbing down the field to another Panther. Jessi intercepted it and zoomed toward the Panthers' side of the field. A Panthers midfielder raced in front of Jessi and kicked the ball away from her. I watched Jessi bump into her, lose her footing, and fall hard. It looked like she might be injured.

The ref's whistle shrieked for a time-out. Jessi jumped up.

"I'm fine!" she called out. The ref nodded, and the game continued, with the Panthers in control of the ball.

As I watched the Panthers player move toward our defenders, I heard yelling coming from the stands.

"Are you blind?"

"That was a foul!"

"No fair!"

I glanced back at the stands. It was hard to tell who was yelling, but it sounded like Kicks parents—which was weird, because Kicks parents were not normally the yelling kind.

I saw Zarine glance at the stands too, distracted by the yelling. And that was when a Panthers player sent the ball whizzing past her into the goal.

Cheers erupted from the Panthers side of the field. On the Kicks side I actually heard boos!

"Okay, don't worry, girls!" Coach Flores called. "Just keep your eyes on the ball!"

So that was exactly what I did. Grace got control of the ball. She passed it to me, and I drove it toward the goal. I saw Hailey open, so I passed it to her. She raced up really close to the goal and then lobbed it high, over the goalie's head.

The ref's whistle blew for our goal, and I high-fived Hailey as we hustled back to our positions.

Fifteen minutes into the game, we were still tied with Pinewood. Coach Flores took out me and Hailey and replaced us with Megan and Brianna. I watched as Mirabelle made two goals, back to back. At the half it was Pinewood 3, Kicks 1.

During our halftime break we heard more yelling from some of the Kicks parents.

"Give it your all!"

"Send them packing!"

I glanced into the stands, trying to figure out who was doing all the yelling. I knew for sure it wasn't my parents. Coach Flores saw me looking.

"Just drown it out," she told me. "I'm going to have a talk with some people after the game. They just don't realize how distracting it is. Not to mention poor sportsmanship."

We all nodded. Coach Flores put Hailey and me back in for the second half. Hailey scored again right away, which was great, but I was itching to kick that ball into the net.

I got a chance about ten minutes into the half. One of the Panthers tried to pass the ball to a teammate, but I intercepted it. I raced down the field, heart pounding. The goalie was ready for me, but I sent the ball skidding across the grass so low that it was a white blur against the green.

"Goal!"

Hailey and I had evened things up. But the Panthers quickly scored another goal. Panthers 4, Kicks 3.

Coach Flores benched us again, and I watched as the

Panthers scored two more times during the second half. Megan scored one more goal for the Kicks, but it wasn't enough.

The game-ending whistle blew, and the Panthers let out a cheer. We lined up and walked across the field and slapped their hands, one by one. When I got to Mirabelle, she was grinning widely.

"Good job," she said when I slapped her hand. "But not good enough."

That stung, and I didn't say anything. When I got to the end of the line, I looked around to find Jessi, to tell her what Mirabelle had said. To my surprise (although I didn't gasp this time), I saw her talking to Coach Darby!

I wanted to wait and ask her what she was doing, but Mom, Dad, and Maisie walked out onto the field.

"Good job, Devin," Mom said.

"Yeah, but not good enough," I mumbled, repeating Mirabelle's words.

"Don't worry. It's only a scrimmage," Maisie said. "It doesn't count."

That didn't make me feel much better. Yes, it was only a scrimmage. But the loss felt like a big letdown after the pep rally. The school had high hopes for us. My grandparents were coming out to see us play our first game—which also happened to be against Pinewood.

The pressure was on!

CHAPTER SEVEN

"Earth to Devin!"

Emma roused me from my worried thoughts by tapping me on the shoulder.

I jumped a little.

"I've been calling you," she said. "We're going to that new burger place, remember? My mom's driving us."

She nodded toward the parking lot, where Mrs. Kim waved from in front of her red minivan. Frida, Zoe, and Jessi were standing next to her.

"Oh yeah, right!" I said, remembering. Usually after a game some or all of the Kicks went out to eat together. Grace had suggested we do it after the scrimmage today.

"Tell your mom thank you for driving," my mom said to Emma as she handed me some cash. "See you back home, Devin."

"Thanks!" I said, and Emma and I ran to join the others.

"Good scrimmage today," Mrs. Kim said as we all climbed in. "You all played very well. I wish I could say the same about some of those people in the stands. So aggressive!"

"Yeah, it was really distracting on the field," I agreed from my seat behind her and Emma.

"Did you notice who was doing it?" Jessi asked.

Mrs. Kim shook her head. "Some parents I didn't recognize started it, and then others joined in. Megan's father has such a loud voice! Adults should know better than to behave that way."

"Coach Flores said she was going to talk to parents about it," Emma informed her, and Mrs. Kim nodded.

"Good!"

She pulled into the parking lot of Bob's Burger Barn.

"I'll pick you up in one hour. Have a good time," she told us.

We all thanked her and headed inside. Most of the other Kicks were in line already, waiting to order their food. Everyone was talking about the game. Grace and Megan were on either side of Hailey.

"Great game today," Grace congratulated her.

"Yeah, we're really lucky you joined the team," Megan said.

Hailey smiled. "Thanks! I'm glad I joined too." She spotted me and nodded her head toward me. "Devin and Jessi really convinced me to do it."

"Well, I'm glad they did," Grace said. "You're our secret weapon."

I felt a little twinge of something . . . not jealousy, exactly. (I had already been through that with Hailey, when I'd thought Steven liked her and didn't like me anymore.) No, it was more of a competitive feeling. I wanted to be the secret weapon. I wanted to be the best player on the Kicks.

"May I take your order?" asked the girl behind the counter, wearing a red-and-white checkered cap.

I looked at the menu and ordered one Barn Buster (barbecue sauce and bacon), with a country lemonade. Within a few minutes we all held trays of food and drinks. Jessi, Emma, Frida, Zoe, and I found a table together and sat down.

"That was one stressful game," Jessi said, taking a bite of her burger.

"That's exactly what I was thinking!" I said. "I mean, the school is expecting us to win. The parents in the stands were putting more pressure on us. And my grandparents are coming to the first game!"

Emma looked puzzled. "Do they like to yell out things at games?"

I shook my head. "No, but I want them to see me win a game. They're coming all the way across the country! It would stink to lose."

Everyone nodded sympathetically.

"Well, I feel anxious about the new you-know-what coming," Jessi said. "I still haven't finished my new room. And those couch cushions are not comfortable!"

"We could help you again on Saturday," Zoe suggested.

"Actually, I had another plan for us on Saturday," Jessi said. "But it all depends if Frida is available. Do you have any auditions, Frida?"

"No," Frida said, a dark look coming across her face. "Talk about pressure. I can't even get any auditions!"

"All this talk about pressure is making me feel pressured," Emma said. "But you're right, Devin. Everyone is expecting us to win this season. I hope we don't let them down!"

"Listen, if we do our best, that's all we can do," Zoe said.

"So you're not feeling stressed too?" I asked her.

Zoe shook her head. "Compared to planning my bat mitzvah, this is nothing," she said.

"That was such a fun party!" Emma said. "We need to look at those pictures again. Maybe we can do that on Saturday."

"I told you, I'm planning something," Jessi said.

I turned to face her. "Okay, you're being very mysterious right now. What's up?"

"I want it to be a surprise," Jessi said. "Just trust me, okay?"

Zoe shrugged. "I trust you."

"Me too," said Emma.

"This better not be one of those let's-cheer-up-Frida things," Frida said, frowning. "I am not in the mood for balloons and clowns and ice cream."

Jessi traced an X across her heart. "I promise. There will be no balloons, or clowns, or ice cream. Although, I don't see what you have against ice cream. That's just wrong."

Frida actually smiled a little, and that was when I realized that I should trust Jessi too.

"All right," I said. "What time do you think it's going to be?"

"Why, do you have other plans?" Jessi asked.

"Actually, I do," I answered. "If I'm going to deal with all this pressure, I've got to push myself to be in top form. I want to get in some extra training."

"That sounds like the exact opposite of what you should do," Emma pointed out.

"This is Devin we're talking about," Jessi said. "If she's not pushing herself, she's not happy."

"That's not true," I said. "Other things make me happy."

"This Barn Buster burger is making me happy," Emma said.

I hadn't even had a bite of mine yet. I took one, and it was delicious.

"This is really good," I agreed.

For now I would have to settle for burger happiness. Tomorrow, I vowed, I would start training harder.

Because even though I hadn't admitted it, I knew Jessi was right! I wasn't happy unless I was pushing myself.

CHAPTER EIGHT

When the alarm went off on my phone the next morning, I groaned and pulled the blankets over my head. I allowed myself one quick moment to feel sorry for myself, then threw the blankets off and sprang out of bed. It was only five thirty, but if I wanted to fit in some extra training time before school, this was what I had to do.

Coach Darby used to say to us when I was on the Griffons, "Somewhere in the world, someone is training when you are not. When you face her on the field, she will win." Now that Coach Darby was the coach for Pinewood, I knew that Mirabelle was getting that same advice. I imagined her getting up early to train too. Maybe she had gotten up even earlier than I had! The drowsiness faded as I hurriedly pulled on my favorite pair of running pants, a sleek, black pair with a bright pink stripe down each side. I thought of them as my racing stripes. I knew it was probably all in my head, but I felt like they made me run faster.

The house was quiet and still. The rest of my family was sleeping as I threw on a tank, pulled my hair back, and started stretching. I put on a Windbreaker and then was out the door. The sun hadn't risen yet, so it was still dark.

My mom used to never let me run before the sun was up. "You could get hit by a car. It's just too dangerous," she would say, even though I begged and pleaded.

Finally she relented after I talked her into buying me a special Windbreaker for joggers. It reflected the light from car headlights, making it way easier for drivers to spot me. Not that there were many cars out this early in the morning. But that's how moms are. They worry.

The other part of the deal for being able to run in the early morning was that I had to keep within a couple blocks of our house, which got boring fast. I was running in circles, passing the same old houses over and over again.

But listening to my inspirational, fast-paced running playlist got me into the groove. As my feet hit the pavement in time to the music, I imagined every step making me faster on the field. To keep the routine exciting, I added some fast sprints every few minutes. I'd jog at my normal pace, then take off racing like a cheetah for a minute or so, before slowing down again. I repeated this throughout my run. Soon the sweat was pouring down my face and the Windbreaker started to feel too hot, but I left it on for safety. And because if my mom caught me running without it, I'd be in big trouble!

As I wiped the sweat off my face, I couldn't stop thinking about how Pinewood had beaten us at that scrimmage. I knew it hadn't been a game, but a win would have gone a long way toward boosting our confidence.

"A strong start leads to a strong finish," Coach Valentine, the boys' coach, had said to us when he'd been filling in for Coach Flores.

Losing to Pinewood in the scrimmage was a weak start, but I decided it didn't count. The official start to the season would be our first game. We'd just have to win in order to set the tone that would carry us to the state championships. I felt the nerves begin to build up in me, thinking of how everyone would be there watching. My grandparents were flying across the country to see me. What if I totally blew it?

I shook my head to clear those negative thoughts. *Relax,* I told myself. *That's why you're doing this extra training. To be the best you can be.*

Then I thought of something Coach Flores always said to all of us Kicks: "Have fun and do your best. I'm so proud of you!"

It made me smile as I turned the corner and jogged back to my house. Coach Flores was so sweet. When I had first joined the Kicks, she hadn't wanted to push her players at all, and the team had suffered because of it. When

Coach had realized that we wanted to win, she'd figured out how to combine her emphasis on fun and fairness with solid coaching skills. It had worked, and the Kicks had started to succeed.

As I walked up the steps to our house, I grabbed the morning newspaper, the *Kentville Chronicle*, on the way inside. There was some stuff on the front page about a big election, but a small picture in the top corner caught my eye. I'd recognize that blue-and-white uniform anywhere. It was my Kicks co-captain, Grace, leaping into the air as her head made contact with the soccer ball. Underneath the picture, it said, *Can the Kicks Do It Again? Page C1*.

When I walked into the house, I could smell coffee brewing in the kitchen, so I knew my dad must have been up. But I couldn't wait to walk even the few feet into the kitchen. I stood in the hall and opened the newspaper, pages falling to my feet as I did so.

On the front of the sports section was the photo of Grace, taken at practice last fall. I eagerly read the article underneath:

> **The middle school spring soccer season is starting, and everyone is wondering if the Kentville Kangaroos will "Kick" their way to the state championships. The Kicks made it into their first play-off season since 1996 this past fall. The success of the team is attributed to a combination of new coaching techniques by Coach Maria Luisa Flores,**

a member of the Kangaroos when they were two-time state champs in 1991 and 1992, and a talented roster of athletes.

"We're having fun, but my girls are serious competitors at the same time," Flores said. "I'm very proud of how well they did."

As for the team's chances of becoming state champs, Flores had this to say: "Anything is possible with a group of girls as talented as this. More important to me is that they learn a lot about themselves, what they're capable of, and what it means to be part of a team."

Sally Lane of Lane's Sporting Goods is one Kentville resident expecting big things from the Kicks. In fact, she has donated new equipment to the team, and will be paying for the resodding of their field after this season is over.

"A team of champions needs a field worthy of them," Lane said. "Lane's Sporting Goods is proud to be a sponsor of the Kicks. I'd be surprised if we got anything less than a spectacular season from this group of players."

"Let's just say that I've been dusting the trophy case that has the 1991 and 1992 state champion trophies in them," Kentville Middle School Principal Santiago Gallegos joked. "I have a feeling we'll be adding another one soon."

The first game of the season will take place at

> noon on March 23 at Pinewood Preparatory School in Pinewood. Admission is free.
>
> "Come on out and cheer our girls on," Principal Gallegos said. "Wear blue and white. Let's show Pinewood that Kentville supports our team and bathe the stands with blue and white. We want this to be the biggest turnout for a non-home game in Kentville middle school soccer history!"

The relaxed feeling I'd had after my run immediately disappeared. I felt the butterflies in my stomach begin tumbling and turning, as if they were in a snow globe someone was shaking really, really hard. The pressure felt even more intense now.

But was I the only one who felt it?

At school practically everybody was buzzing about the article.

"We're famous!" Jessi said gleefully at lunch. She turned toward the table where Grace sat with some of the other eighth-grade players. "Grace! Can I get your autograph?" she yelled.

Grace laughed and waved. Everyone seemed really pumped up about the article. I totally got it, and I thought it was awesome how everyone believed in us. Except, I couldn't help feeling that it put too much of a burden on the Kicks. But no one else seemed to be thinking like that.

I didn't want to be a downer by saying anything. Instead I bottled it up and decided to put that energy into my training routine every day. If I worked as hard as I could, I wouldn't let anyone down. Not Ms. Lane, not Principal Gallegos, not my teammates, and not my grandparents!

There was no soccer practice that Friday afternoon, so when I got home, I took another run around the neighborhood. I was glad that it was light and I didn't have to wear the jacket, because the day was sunny and unseasonably warm.

As I got back to my room, I started searching for online workouts to add to my routine. I found this high-intensity exercise video where you worked out at maximum intensity for twenty seconds, then rested for ten seconds. It began with burpees. That's a move that you start by squatting. Then you put your hands on the ground and kick your feet back to form a plank position. Next you do a push-up, return to the squat, and stand up and jump. I did it as fast as I could along with the video. Squat, kick to plank, push up, squat, stand, jump. I did it over and over. Twenty seconds doesn't sound like a long time, but it started to feel like an eternity, especially when I was on the fourth round. When the ten-second rest came, I sprawled out, panting, on the floor of my room. That was when I heard a chime on my computer—someone was trying to video chat with me. I looked up and saw that it was Kara.

I heaved myself into my desk chair, puffing as I accepted her request. Her face popped up on the screen, smiling until she got a good look at me. Then she gasped in horror.

"Devin! What's wrong?" she asked, concerned. "Are you sick?"

I could see myself in the chat screen. My face was bright red and I was sweating. Hair had escaped from my ponytail and hung in wet clumps next to my face.

"Ugh!" I said as my hand flew to my face, tucking the wet strands of hair behind my ears. "I'm not sick. I just got back from a run, and then I was doing a round of burpees."

Kara wrinkled her nose in disgust.

"'I love burpees,' said no one ever," she said. "Why are you torturing yourself with those?"

I grabbed the bottle of water on my desk and took a chug before answering.

"It's the spring soccer season," I told her. "We've got our first game in a couple of weeks. I want to win."

Kara looked at me, her eyes narrowing in suspicion. "You always want to win," she said. "What makes this so different that you're running and doing burpees? Something else is up. My best-friend sense is tingling. Fess up, Devin."

I took a deep breath, and then everything came spilling out of me.

"There's so much pressure on us this time!" I confided, glad to have Kara to talk to. "When I first joined the Kicks, no one cared if we won or lost. Besides the people on the team, hardly anyone knew we even existed. Now everyone is expecting us to be phenomenal—like state-champ-level phenomenal. This lady even donated new equipment and is fixing up our cruddy field for us."

I grabbed the towel I had tossed onto the floor and mopped the sweat from my head. I didn't know what was making me sweat more, all the exercise or all the stress.

"And the principal invited the entire town to our first game," I continued. "But that's not all. My grandpa and grandma are flying in for a visit, and they'll be at the game too. So if we lose, we lose spectacularly and in front of everyone we know!"

I slid down in the chair, the weight of everything pushing me down.

"Oh, Devin," Kara sighed. "Why do you have to be so hard on yourself?"

I shook my head. "It's not me. Everyone is expecting so much!"

"You're the one who always expects the most," Kara insisted. "It's both a blessing and a curse. It's what makes you such a great athlete and competitor. You're always ready to go that extra step. But then sometimes it can just eat you up, like it's doing now. You've got to give yourself a break. All you can do is your best. Anything after that is out of your control. And you have to remember, it's just one game."

My ears were hearing what Kara was saying and transmitting it to my brain. But my brain was being stubborn. It didn't want to believe that everything was going to be okay, or that I shouldn't be too hard on myself. All it wanted to know was that my team was going to win!

CHAPTER NINE

Even though spilling my guts to Kara had made me feel a teeny bit better, I still got up early the next morning to get another run in before Jessi and her mom picked me up. It was Saturday. We were finally going to find out what Jessi's mysterious plan was to help Frida!

When I climbed into Mrs. Dukes's van, Jessi, Emma, and Zoe were inside.

"Next stop: Frida's house," Jessi announced. "Then we'll see if my plan works."

"Will you tell us now?" I pleaded.

Emma shook her head. "We've been trying to get it out of her, but she won't say a word."

When Frida got into the van, she looked apprehensive.

"I'm trusting you completely, Jessi," she said. "If there is a clown anywhere, I'll freak."

"But clowns are so cute!" Emma insisted.

Zoe shuddered. "They give me the creeps."

As we debated the pros and cons of clowns, Mrs. Dukes pulled up in front of a long, L-shaped building. It looked vaguely familiar. I had been here before. I just couldn't place it.

"Wait a minute," I said as the memory came back to me. "Is this Lavender Hills?"

"What's Lavender Hills?" Frida asked suspiciously.

"It's a place where a very interesting person lives," Jessi said, still being mysterious. "She might be able to help you."

We walked along the brick pathway leading to the front door.

"It's an adult care home," I explained. "You know, where they take care of old people."

Emma, Zoe, and Frida exchanged questioning glances.

"What are we doing here?" Frida asked. "And have you been here before, Devin?"

Jessi nodded. "We both have, when we were on the Griffons. Coach Darby took us here for a team building exercise. Her mom lives here. We played games with the residents."

"Aha!" I exclaimed. "So that's what you were talking to Coach Darby about at the Pinewood scrimmage."

"Yep." Jessi smiled.

"I don't understand. How will this help me?" Frida asked, totally confused.

"When we were here with the Griffons, Devin and I got

to hang out with Coach Darby's mom, Mrs. Darby," Jessi explained. "But I also got a chance to meet Mrs. Darby's best friend, Miriam. She was so cool and funny. And it also happens that she used to be a movie star!"

"A movie star? What movies was she in?" Frida was intrigued.

Jessi shrugged. "I don't know. She's, like, really old. So they were definitely before our time. But she's someone who knows about what it's like to be in show business. I think she'll be the perfect person to give you some advice, Frida."

We rang the doorbell and were buzzed inside. Jessi gave our names at the desk and said we were there to visit Miriam Hall. The receptionist gave us guest badges that we hung around our necks.

"Mrs. Hall is waiting for you in the community room," she said, pointing to an open doorway at the end of the corridor.

We went inside, and there were a bunch of elderly people sitting at tables and on couches and chairs scattered around the room. At one table next to a large picture window sat an elderly woman with dyed bright red hair. Jessi made a beeline toward her.

"Hello, Mrs. Hall," Jessi said. "It's me, Jessi. Thanks for agreeing to meet with us."

"Please, darling, call me Miriam," she replied. Her face was very wrinkled, and she had on bright red lipstick and blue eye shadow. She wore loose black pants with a blue shirt, topped with a floral, long-sleeve kimono-style sweater. It had fringes on the edges that fluttered as she moved her arms.

"Sit, sit," she said as she motioned to the chairs around the table. We all introduced ourselves. "So what brings you here today, my darlings?" she asked, arching an eyebrow at us.

"She's an actor," Jessi said, pointing at Frida. "And she's been having some problems. I thought you might be able to help."

Miriam looked at Frida, appraising her. "So you have the calling, do you, my dear?" Miriam asked. "It's both a blessing and a curse."

A blessing and a curse! That was what Kara had said to me about my competitive nature. I guessed that soccer and acting had more in common that I'd thought.

"Right now it's more of a curse," Frida confided to Miriam. Then she told Miriam everything, about her starring role in *Mall Mania* and how she couldn't get any more parts.

"So basically I'm a has-been at thirteen!" Frida ended with a wail.

Miriam laughed. Loudly. Her deep, rich chuckle echoed throughout the community room.

"Your career is just beginning, my silly little child," Miriam said once she had stopped laughing. "Why, if I had given up the many times I had been rejected, I would never have worked a day!"

"Were you in movies?" Frida asked.

Miriam nodded. "Many. But it didn't come easily. I had to work and hustle to get those parts, especially the first few. I even lied a few times. Sometimes that worked, but sometimes it backfired. Like the time I said I was a terrific swimmer, so I could get a part in an Esther Williams movie. Of course, I didn't know how! I sank to the bottom of the pool like a rock. One of the crew had to dive in to save me. Otherwise I would have drowned. Of course I was fired after that, but I didn't give up."

"Who is Esther Williams?" Zoe wondered. I had never heard of her either, so I was glad Zoe asked.

"She was a champion swimmer and an actor," Frida explained. "She made 'aquamusical' movies popular. They featured synchronized swimming and diving to music."

"Very good." Miriam nodded approvingly at Frida. "You know the history of your craft. That's very important. So many young people don't bother."

Frida beamed under Miriam's praise, but then she wrinkled her forehead. "Esther Williams was a star in the 1940s and 50s. That means you'd have to be . . ."

"As old as dirt!" Miriam supplied with a chuckle. "I'm ninety years old. I got my first movie role in 1947. I was twenty years old."

"Wow!" Emma's eyes were huge. "Ninety years old!"

"I should sell tickets for people to come and look at me," Miriam said.

Emma's cheeks turned red. "I'm sorry. I didn't mean to—"

Miriam laughed again, her deep, rich chuckle.

"I wish it were something to brag about, but around here"—Miriam waved her arms—"nonagenarians are a dime a dozen. That's the word they use for old coots who are in their nineties."

This time we all laughed. Miriam was so funny. She might have looked old, but she didn't act it.

"One time," Miriam continued, "I got let go from a movie because the leading man didn't like it that I was taller than him. Another time the director wouldn't hire me because he said my feet were too big. I didn't let any of that stop me. I kept going. Not everyone is going to like you. In this business you've got to like yourself. Otherwise this business will destroy you."

When Miriam asked one of the aides to bring us all lemonade, Frida took her phone out and started furiously typing on it.

"You starred in more than three dozen movies?" Frida asked, shocked. "Some with Lauren Bacall, Bette Davis, Cary Grant, and Humphrey Bogart?"

I didn't recognize most of those names, but from Frida's tone I could tell they must have been really big stars.

"I did indeed." Miriam nodded. "The stories I could tell you! You'll have to come back for another visit. It's almost lunchtime, and I like to take a nap after I eat."

Frida stared at Miriam with awe. She was clearly

starstruck. "Will you be my new best friend forever?" Frida asked her.

"Darling, at my age I can't promise forever," Miriam said, and then chuckled. "But you can come and visit me anytime you want."

As we left Lavender Hills, Frida was unnaturally quiet. But unlike after that disastrous soccer practice when she wouldn't say anything, this time was different. Her eyes were shining and her cheeks were glowing.

"I can't believe it," she murmured, more to herself than to us. "She's a living legend. And I got to meet her!"

Zoe put an arm around Jessi and smiled up at her.

"That was a great idea," she said.

Frida suddenly launched herself at Jessi.

"Aaaarrrggghhh!" Jessi cried as Frida almost knocked her over.

Frida wrapped her arms around Jessi and hugged her tight. "Thank you, thank you!" she said. Frida's auburn hair glowed in the sunshine, and it reminded me of someone.

"Hey, don't you think Frida will be a lot like Miriam when she's ninety?" I asked.

Everyone laughed as Frida untangled herself from Jessi.

"I hope so, darlings," Frida said, before imitating Miriam's chuckle perfectly. We were all cracking up as we got into Mrs. Dukes's van.

"What's so funny?" Mrs. Dukes asked. "I could use a laugh. I stopped at Lullabies to see if the stroller I wanted was in stock, but the salesperson said they no longer carry it."

"Don't worry. Jessi can carry the baby around for you everywhere," Emma joked.

Mrs. Dukes glanced in the rearview mirror and beamed at Jessi, who was sitting next to me in the very back of the van.

"Jessi is going to be such a good big sister," Mrs. Dukes said, smiling. "But I wouldn't ask her to do that!"

I looked at Jessi, expecting her to make some kind of joke, but her face fell. She looked upset.

"What's wrong?" I whispered to her as Frida started telling Mrs. Dukes about meeting Miriam.

Jessi took a deep breath, and her lower lip trembled.

"It's just," she whispered, and then she bit her lip to keep it from quaking. "It's just . . . I have no idea how to be a big sister! What if I totally screw it up? What if I'm the worst sister in the entire history of sisters?"

Poor Jessi! Just when Frida was feeling better, now Jessi was all worried. Jessi had helped Frida. But what could I do to help Jessi?

Chapter Ten

Beep! Beep! Beep!

I won't say I sprang right out of bed at five thirty on Tuesday morning, but after four days of my early routine, I was a little more used to it. I suited up and headed outside to run around—and around and around—my neighborhood.

The running-in-circles part was starting to get to me more than the early wake-ups. So that was probably why, when I passed that pink concrete wall in front of the house on Palmetto Court, I decided to mix up my routine.

Maybe you've seen videos of those guys who do parkour, jumping on top of things and somersaulting in the air and stuff as they make their way around a city? Well, I didn't have anything as crazy as that planned. But when I saw the wall, which was maybe four feet high, I thought, *I should jump onto that wall and then run across it and jump back down*.

Sounds easy, right? And it should have been, except that

when I jumped on top of the wall, I led with my right leg, and when I landed on top, I felt a jolt of pain hit my right calf. I ran across the wall, limping. Then I jumped down and stopped, hands on my knees.

I had pulled a muscle. At least that was what it felt like.

Smart move, Devin! I scolded myself. *That's what you get for being bored!*

I jogged home, feeling pain in my right leg the whole way. I was really mad at myself. We had another scrimmage that afternoon—this time with the Riverdale Rams, another one of our big rivals.

"How was your run, Devin?" Dad asked, sipping his coffee as I walked through the front door.

"Fine," I mumbled, and I headed up the stairs to shower.

"Are you limping?" he called after me, but I didn't answer him.

I couldn't be hurt! Not today. I jumped into the shower, and the hot water felt good. Too good, because soon Mom was knocking on the door.

"Devin, you're running late—and wasting water!" she called.

I ended the shower and quickly got dressed. When I got downstairs, Mom and Dad had their eyes focused on me.

"Devin, Dad says you might have hurt yourself on your run?" Mom asked.

I shook my head. "No, I'm fine," I lied, but only because I did not want to admit to anyone that I was hurt—not even to myself. If I kept telling myself I was fine, I would be.

Mom raised an eyebrow. "Well, okay, honey. I know

you're very focused this season, but just don't push yourself too hard."

"I won't," I promised, even though it was probably already too late.

I tried my best not to limp all day at school, and nobody even noticed. We had a health lesson in gym class, so I didn't have to worry there. By the time school was over and we were on the bus to Riverdale, I was feeling a lot better.

"Think we can beat Riverdale?" Jessi asked me.

"We beat them before," I told her, which was true—even though they had tried their best to sabotage us. I realized my foot was anxiously tapping on the bus floor as I talked. I couldn't wait for this game!

The bus pulled up to the Riverdale field, dotted with Rams in their red-and-yellow uniforms kicking the ball around. We piled out of the bus and made our way to the away-team side.

On the way, we passed a Rams player with long, blond hair—Jamie Quinn. Jessi and I had first met Jamie when she'd orchestrated her team's sabotage attempts against the Kicks. I hadn't liked her very much then, for good reason, but I'd gotten to know her better when we'd both been on the Griffons winter league team. We had become friends, kind of, but I wondered if she was going to have the same attitude as Mirabelle, now that we were back on opposing teams.

But Jamie actually smiled when she saw us, and gave us a nod.

"Good luck today," she said, and then went back to her drills. Jessi and I looked at each other.

"Looks like we're still on Jamie's good side," I said.

"That's nice," Jessi said. "But I still want to beat them!"

And so did I. We did our sock swap and warmed up, and with every minute I got more and more pumped up for the game. I was feeling pretty good because nobody had noticed that I was still limping a little bit. If Coach Flores thought I was injured, she wouldn't let me play.

Coach Flores put me in to start, along with Grace and Hailey as forwards. Grace got control of the ball when the whistle blew, and we raced down the field. Grace and Hailey passed the ball back and forth, and Hailey took a shot at the goal, but the goalie jumped and caught it.

We went back and forth down the field a few times, with neither team scoring. My leg was starting to hurt again. I gained control of the ball midfield and passed it to Grace—or at least I tried to. My leg twisted funny as I kicked, and the ball went skidding to Jamie on the Rams! It was like I had passed it right to her.

Jessi was on Jamie like a monster and got the ball back from her, but I was still mortified. I hadn't made a mistake like that since, like, third grade. Coach Flores called a time out and waved me over.

"Devin, is there something up with your right leg?" she asked. "You're limping."

I couldn't keep up the lie. "I think I pulled a muscle this morning," I admitted.

Coach nodded. "Take the bench then, Devin. I don't want you to hurt yourself any more than you already are."

Tears stung my eyes as I went to the bench. And I

couldn't even tell myself that it wasn't fair, because it was my own fault!

The game started back up, and I sat down next to Emma.

"Devin, are you okay?" she asked.

"Just a pulled muscle," I mumbled.

"I'm sorry!" Emma said, hugging me. "But don't worry. We can still beat the Rams. Frida is back to her old self!"

She pointed to the field, where Frida was glued to a Rams player trying to get past her.

"Are you ready for your close-up?" Frida yelled, lunging toward the Rams player and kicking the ball away from her.

"Wow!" I said. "So, who's she channeling this time?"

"I think Miriam," Emma answered. "She's been using actor terms. Like, I just heard her tell one of the Rams that it was time for her curtain call."

I smiled a little then. Frida was a true original. "Whatever works!" I said.

It was tough watching the game from the bench. Despite Frida's best efforts, Jamie scored a goal right before the half ended. Then, when the second half started, the Rams scored again right away.

That was when the Kicks parents started yelling.

"Look alive out there, defense!"

"Wake up, goalie!"

I looked over at the goal, and Zarine looked like she might cry. So she wasn't on her game when the next Rams player came charging toward the goal and lobbed one in over her head.

And that was when Coach Flores lost it—for the first

time ever. She turned toward the stands.

"Parents, please knock it off!" she yelled. "This is NOT helping!"

The Kicks were all stunned—and so were the parents, because Coach Flores never got upset and never yelled. That quieted down the parents, and the Kicks were more focused after that. Jessi scored, so it was Rams 3, Kicks 1.

Right after that Hailey got a ball past the Rams' goalie, making it a 3–2 game. For the newest member of the team, Hailey was excelling. Usually I was happy about that. Everyone on the Kicks needed to be at their best in order for us to win. Yet it was a lot easier to be happy when I was playing, not benched on the sidelines, watching Hailey making a goal that could have been mine. Yet I pushed those feelings aside and cheered. We had a chance to win this!

But the Rams fought back hard. Coach Flores had put Emma on goal, and the Rams got two balls past her before the final whistle blew. The Rams had won the scrimmage. It wasn't that Emma had been playing badly either; their offense had plowed through our defense.

Poor Emma looked really upset as we lined up to congratulate the Rams. I didn't feel much better than she looked. The bus ride back to Kentville was a quiet one.

I knew we were all thinking the same thing. Yes, it had been only a scrimmage. But so far the Kicks were not looking like a championship team.

CHAPTER ELEVEN

A couple of days later Jessi, Emma, Zoe, Frida, and I were in the noisy school cafeteria, eating lunch.

"So you guys will help me finish the room tomorrow, right?" Jessi asked. "The paint is dry, and my new bed came. My new, teeny tiny bed for my teeny tiny room." She sighed.

"Of course we'll help you!" Emma said.

"So do you get to decorate it any way you want?" Zoe asked.

"I could put a disco ball and a chocolate fountain in there, and Mom and Dad wouldn't notice," Jessi replied. "All they talk about is the baby." She looked down at her salad and started pushing the lettuce around with her fork.

Emma gasped. "You said 'baby'!"

"I've given up," Jessi said sadly. "Pretty soon it's going to be all baby, baby, baby anyway."

She put down her fork. "Gotta go to the girls' room. BRB."

"Wow, she seems really bummed about this baby," Zoe remarked.

"Probably jealous," Frida guessed. "She's been the center of attention for all these years."

"That might be part of it," I said. "But I also know that she's worried about being a big sister. She thinks she doesn't know how."

Emma frowned. "Poor Jessi. She'll be a great big sister. It just comes naturally. It's not like you need to take a class in being a big sister."

"Well, they do have babysitting classes," Zoe pointed out.

I nodded. "I know. I took one back in Connecticut." As I said the words, an idea came to me. "I think I know how we can help Jessi!"

I leaned in and whispered my idea to my friends. We finished just as Jessi walked back up.

She raised an eyebrow. "What, were you guys talking about me?"

"Just talking about how cool we're going to make your new room," Zoe replied smoothly.

That seemed to satisfy Jessi, and she sat down and we all finished our lunch. I was a little distracted, thinking about our surprise for Jessi. Friday night was going to be interesting!

We didn't have practice on Friday afternoon, so we all went to Jessi's house after school, at about four. Each one of us had a backpack with us. Zoe and Emma each had a box filled with stuff too.

Jessi greeted us at the door. "Come on in! Mom's making spaghetti for dinner, but we can get started on the room." Then she stopped. "Whoa, Frida, your hair looks cool!"

I looked at Frida. I hadn't noticed, but Jessi was right. Frida's auburn hair was totally different from usual. Her hair was kind of swooped back off her forehead, and then it cascaded down the left side of her head in waves.

"Do you like it?" she asked. "Miriam had this hairstyle in *Treasure of the Lost Cavern*. I thought it was pretty chic."

"Very chic," Zoe agreed.

"Come on," Jessi said. "Let me show you the room so far."

We followed Jessi to her room. It looked much better than the last time we'd seen it. The walls had been painted a nice blue, and the bed had a cute blue bedspread with white stripes. But there were still boxes and bags of stuff stacked up against the wall.

"Not bad," Zoe said. "First we need to organize you. Then we can decorate."

We put down our backpacks and boxes and got to work. Zoe was an organizing whiz, and she barked out orders to us.

"Don't fold the T-shirts. Roll them! They'll fit better in the dresser."

"Books on the bottom shelf of the built-in bookcase. Save the top shelves for electronic equipment!"

"Bulky sweatshirts in the under-the-bed box!"

Before we knew it, the room looked well organized.

"Thanks, guys," Jessi said. "This is awesome!"

"But bland," Emma said. She reached into the box she had brought. "Don't worry. Zoe and I came prepared."

Emma pulled out a blue pillow with turquoise wavy lines. Then she placed it on Jessi's bed. "Perfect!"

Zoe took out a string of blue-and-white lights and started to string them on the wall above Jessi's bed.

"Oh my gosh, this stuff is awesome!" Jessi said. "Where did you get it?"

"It's the benefit of having lots of brothers and sisters between us," Emma replied. "We always get lots of cast-offs."

Frida, Jessi, and I watched as Emma and Zoe added finishing touches—a metal desk lamp, a chalkboard in a white frame, and finally, from Zoe, a framed picture of all of us from her bat mitzvah. She placed it on Jessi's dresser.

"Voila!" she cried. "Now this looks like a room."

Jessi looked like she was almost going to cry. "Wow, guys. This is beautiful. Thank you! No more sleeping in the living room!"

Jessi's dad walked up to us then. "Girls, time for dinner!"

We followed him to the dining room and sat down for a meal of spaghetti, meatballs, garlic bread, and salad. I didn't realize how hungry I was until the plate of spaghetti was in front of me.

"You girls are so wonderful to help Jessi with her room," Mrs. Dukes said. "We can't thank you enough."

"It was fun!" Emma said. "But not as much fun as what we're going to do after dinner." Then she put her hand over her mouth. "Whoops! I think that was supposed to be a surprise."

Jessi looked right at me. "What kind of surprise?"

"It will be fun, I promise," I said. "See, I used to take babysitting classes in Connecticut. So I thought we could have a little babysitting class here, after dinner."

Jessi's eyes narrowed. "What kind of class?"

I put my napkin in front of my mouth. "Diapers," I mumbled.

"I'm sorry, what did you say?" Jessi asked.

"Diapers," I said, a little more loudly.

"Gross!" Jessi wailed. "Anything but diapers, please!"

"It'll be fun!" Emma said. "Devin brought tiny diapers, and we all brought our old baby dolls."

"Well, I never had a baby doll, so I brought my stuffed *T. rex*," Zoe explained.

"A stuffed *T. rex* in a diaper?" Jessi asked. "Okay then, I've got to see this."

"What a cute idea, girls!" Mrs. Duke said, and then she started to cry a little. "Jessi is so lucky to have such good friends."

Jessi leaned over and whispered to me, "Mom cries all the time now. She says it's hormones."

We finished dinner and helped clear the table.

"Okay, everybody, it's diaper training time!" I announced.

Jessi groaned as we piled into her new stylish but tiny room. I opened my backpack and took out two dolls—Baby Sissy, my childhood doll, and Maisie's beloved doll, Baby Tina. (I had borrowed it without asking her, which I knew could be disastrous, but it was for a good cause, I reasoned.) Then I took out some newborn diapers Mom had bought for me once I'd told her we were helping Jessi.

I gave Baby Tina to Jessi and passed out the diapers. Frida and Emma both had taken out their baby dolls, and Zoe was clutching her green *T. rex*.

"Baby dolls always scared me when I was little," Zoe said defensively. "But Mr. T-Rex is super-cuddly-wuddly."

"And now Mr. Cuddly Wuddly needs a diaper," I said. "Okay, if this were a real diaper situation, we would put a towel on the bed first. Accidents happen when you least expect it."

Jessi grimaced. "Oh, I'm expecting it."

"So, you lay the diaper out flat like this," I said, demonstrating on Jessi's bed. "And then you place the baby on top of the diaper, and then you attach the tabs here, and here."

I snugly wrapped the diaper around Baby Sissy. Emma and Frida did the same with their babies, and Zoe got the diaper on Mr. T-Rex. Jessi seemed reluctant, but she started to put the diaper on Baby Tina.

Zoe moved Mr. T-Rex up and down. "I'm Mr. T-Rex, and I made a wee-wee!" she said in a deep dinosaur voice.

Frida started talking in a TV-commercial voice. "Did

your dino make a doo-doo? Then Dino Diapers are what you need. They're prehistorically awesome!"

We were all giggling by then. Jessi held up Baby Tina. "Finished! Are we done now?"

"You did a great job," I said. "You'll make a really good big sister, Jessi."

"Big deal. I can diaper a doll," Jessi said. "Real baby diapers are totally gross. And then what do you do when a baby cries, and screams, and won't stop?"

I started thinking about when Maisie was a baby. She was a crying machine! I wasn't sure how to answer Jessi.

Emma's phone beeped then, and she looked at the screen. "It's from Mom," she said, and then she broke into a grin. "Jessi, I know how you can test your babysitting skills for real! What are you doing tomorrow night?"

"Um, I don't know. I guess being surprised by my well-meaning friends again?" Jessi guessed.

"Yes!" Emma shrieked. "This one will be good, Jessi. And no diapers—well, maybe no diapers. I'm not sure."

"Well, I'm sure," Jessi said. "No diapers!"

"Except for dinosaurs!" Zoe said, in Mr. T-Rex's voice, and we all burst out giggling again.

CHAPTER TWELVE

On Saturday I slept in instead of going for another early run. I had soccer practice that morning, but that wasn't the only reason I slept in. Since pulling the muscle in my leg, I had stopped all the extra training. I didn't want to risk hurting myself again.

I knew it was the right decision, but it was still frustrating, especially when I thought of Mirabelle, who was determined to get that soccer scholarship. She was probably training morning, noon, and night so she could beat us at our first game of the season.

I also thought of Hailey. We both played the same position—striker. I was used to starting in almost every game. Would my lack of training cause me to fall behind and make Hailey be the star striker?

I felt relieved when I jogged onto the soccer field that morning, because my leg felt much better. Other than an occasional twinge, I was almost back to normal.

Yet Coach wasn't taking any chances.

"Devin, you walk," Coach Flores told me as the rest of the Kicks did warm-up laps around the field.

"But, Coach!" I protested. "I'm feeling much better."

"And we want to keep you that way," Coach Flores said firmly. "No arguments."

I walked the perimeter of the soccer field as my teammates, especially Hailey, literally ran circles around me. I felt the butterflies churn in my stomach again. Hailey was fast. A lot faster than I had ever noticed before. *Is she faster than me?* I thought anxiously.

It got worse when Coach had us do a juggling drill.

"Devin, this is all footwork. I know this is hard for you," she said kindly, "but I want to make sure that muscle has time to rest before you start stressing it again, so you're going to sit this one out."

I gave a frustrated groan, and I might have stomped a little as I turned away from Coach to sit on the sidelines as the rest of my team worked. I wasn't proud of myself for acting like that, but I couldn't help it. I felt like I was in one of those dreams where you try to run but you can't. Instead it was like I wanted to play soccer but I couldn't. It wasn't a dream. It was a nightmare!

So I was going to have to sit trapped on the sidelines while the Kicks worked on juggling, kicking the soccer ball repeatedly, and keeping it in the air and not letting it hit the ground. The Kicks would hit the balls with their feet, knees, and even shins or thighs. Juggling was a great way to improve coordination and timing.

"Today you're going to juggle the ball between your left foot and your right foot. We'll change up the routine as we go. Don't worry if you drop the ball," Coach Flores shouted encouragingly. "Pick it up and go right back to it."

Everyone grabbed a ball out of the bags and got started. Thanks to Sally Lane, we now had enough balls to go around. In the past we'd had to take turns for an exercise like this. Not anymore.

Jessi was a great juggler. She hit the ball with the top of her right foot, then the top of her left, speeding up with each tap as she passed the ball back and forth effortlessly between her two feet.

Zarine and Giselle lost the ball a couple of times, while Grace and Anna had a good pace going.

My feet began impatiently tapping on the grass, imaging I was juggling too.

"Now the right foot only," Coach said, and everyone began batting the ball up and down on their right foot.

"Left only!" was met with groans, because for most players the left foot was weaker than the right.

Emma dropped the ball a bunch of times and gave an exaggerated sigh. "This is too hard!"

I watched (okay, I'll admit it, a little jealously) as Hailey handled the ball like a pro, even with her left foot. She was really good.

"Now we're going to have some fun," Coach Flores

said, and smiled. "We're going to increase the number of times you juggle with each foot every time you switch feet. Hit it once on the right, then twice on the left, then three times on the right, then four times on the left. Keep it going as high as you can!"

Everyone shouted encouragingly to their teammates as they tried to add in as many taps as they could without dropping the ball. It looked like fun, and I felt more miserable than ever having to sit it out.

Hailey kept the juggling going, adding on tap after tap. It got harder as she went. Most everyone had dropped out and lost their ball by then, and a crowd gathered to watch. *Oh, great,* I couldn't help thinking, *not only is she an awesome striker, but she's a pro juggler too.*

"I think she's going to set a record," Grace said admiringly.

"That is some fancy footwork," Brianna added.

Hailey shifted slightly as she worked to hold on to the ball. Her control was excellent.

Everyone chanted as Hailey did more and more reps. "One, two, three, four, five, six, seven, eight, nine, ten, eleven, twelve . . ."

Hailey lost control, and the ball bounced away from her as my teammates clapped and cheered. "That's how you do it!" Jessi shouted.

"Awesome, Hailey!" Coach Flores said. "You're the Kicks' juggling expert."

Hailey blushed with pleasure at all the praise she was

receiving. "Thanks," she said as she smiled. "I've been practicing."

Humph. I crossed my arms over my chest. *Maybe I could have gone further than Hailey if I had been allowed to participate,* I thought. I had been working on my juggling too.

I had a big-time case of the grumpies, and it didn't help when Coach Flores broke us into two teams for a scrimmage and made me play goalie.

"I don't want you running too much today, Devin," she said.

I tried not to stomp as I made my way to the goalposts, but maybe I did—just a tiny bit. We had a game in a week, and I wasn't getting the practice I needed. A little voice in my head reminded me that the injury was my own fault for pushing myself too hard. *But I'm feeling better,* another voice replied. *Coach should let me play!*

I don't know if the grouchies were contagious or what, but the happy mood from the juggling drill left the field. The other Kicks seemed tense and nervous during the scrimmage, and started making mistakes.

"Megan, pay attention!" Grace yelled as Megan missed the pass Grace had sent to her.

Then Brianna had a perfect shot at the goal, but her kick veered way off.

"If we play like this against Pinewood, we're toast," Anna complained.

Maybe I wasn't the only one feeling the anxiety before

the upcoming game. During our cool-down before practice ended, I talked to Grace.

"How are you feeling about next week's game?" I asked, trying to sound casual, but inside I couldn't wait to hear if she was feeling the same pressure I was. Grace was usually so cool and calm. To know she might be feeling the same way I did would make me feel less alone.

At first Grace focused only on strategy. "The Pinewood forwards got through our defense time and again during the scrimmage. We've got to beef it up and come up with a good approach for our defenders to take."

I nodded. "I agree. But how do you *feel?*" I asked, emphasizing the word. "Are you nervous?"

Grace pressed her lips together before nodding. "The last two scrimmages didn't go our way. And then after that article ran in the paper . . ." She trailed off before she got her thoughts together. "Well, it's not only me. A lot of the eighth graders are feeling pressured. This is our last year on the Kicks. We don't want to be almost-champions. We want to win!"

I let out a huge sigh of relief, glad to hear that I wasn't the only one who felt that way.

"Me too," I revealed. "The newspaper, the pep rally, Ms. Lane donating all that stuff, plus the principal telling the entire town to come to the game. My grandparents are even flying out for it. It would be horrible to lose!"

Grace nodded, and Giselle, who had been stretching with the other players nearby, joined in the conversation.

"It would be so embarrassing!" she said. "I bet Sally Lane will change her mind about giving us that new sod."

Jessi jumped up from her seated hamstring stretch and wagged a finger at us. "No sod for you, losers!" she joked.

We all laughed a bit, and it broke the tension. But then our faces grew serious again.

"It doesn't help how loud the parents have been at the games either," Anjali admitted.

"It's getting kind of intense," Zoe shared.

"If we lost after we got built up so much by everyone, it would be humiliating," Grace said as Giselle nodded. "We're going to have to make sure we play our best."

Now it was clear that I wasn't the only one feeling stressed. I didn't know if this was a good thing or a bad thing. Maybe the Kicks would be able to take the strain we were under and turn it to our advantage, letting it motivate us. Or—and I shuddered at this thought—would we self-destruct, with the entire town watching?

CHAPTER THIRTEEN

That night I was ready to take a break from worrying about the upcoming game, and I tried to get into a good mood as my dad dropped me and Jessi off at Emma's house.

"I don't think I'll ever get used to this," Dad remarked when we drove up the circular, palm-tree-lined driveway with a big fountain in the middle. Emma's house was really more like a mansion than a normal house. It was so big that the inside was like a maze. When we first became friends, I got lost more than once. It was very intimidating.

With such a fancy house, you would think that Emma's family might be uptight or snooty or something. But they were exactly the opposite—everyone was as nice as Emma, and they made me feel very comfortable whenever I went to visit Emma. It wasn't long before I'd learned how to find my way to the fancy, inground pool and deluxe movie room!

We usually hung out in those places or in Emma's room. But tonight was different.

"My mom's having a girls' night in with her cousins and friends tonight," Emma had revealed to us Friday night at Jessi's house. "But some of her friends wouldn't have been able to make it because they needed babysitters. Mom asked if I would do it, and I figured it would be the perfect practice for Jessi!"

At first Jessi had wrinkled her nose at the thought. "How old are these kids? Do they wear diapers?"

"Sophia and Lily are two-year-olds, and Mason is almost three," Emma had said. "So yes, they are still in diapers, although Mason might be potty-training now."

"Potty-training!" Jessi had shuddered. "The horrors never end, do they? Fine. I'll do it. But not alone. Who else is coming?"

Frida had an audition after practice, and Zoe had plans with her family, so that left me, Emma, and Jessi on toddler patrol.

When we got inside, Emma ushered us into the lower level of the house to a room I had never been inside before—the playroom. The big, open space had brightly painted cubby shelves all around the walls that were filled with toys and books. In the middle of the room were small, round tables with tiny stools, perfect for little ones to sit on. There was a forest mural on one wall, with woodland creatures peeking out from behind trees and flowers.

"Wow!" I said. "It's like a preschool classroom."

"I had a lot of fun times down here," Emma said. "When my brothers and I got older, my dad wanted to convert this into a wine cellar. But my mom has such a big family, and there are so many little kids, that she convinced him to keep it. And we still use it. It comes in handy during family parties. It's completely childproof, so that will make our job easier."

Jessi shook her head as she put her hands over her face. "This is my life now."

Emma slung an arm over her shoulder. "Cheer up! It's not so bad."

I spied something in one of the cubbies and pulled out a stuffed toy of one of the Sunshine Puppies. I rubbed it against Jessi's cheek.

"You make my tail wag when skies are gray," I sang the theme song in a silly voice, trying to imitate the Sunshine Puppies.

Jessi looked up and smiled. "Ray!" she said, grabbing the toy from me. "Ray was always my favorite. Maybe this place isn't so bad."

Just then the sound of a screeching baby echoed through the room as the door opened. In walked Emma's mom and four other women. Three of them were each holding a toddler, but the fourth was carrying two—twins!

"I hope you girls don't mind two extra," Mrs. Kim said as the women put the babies down on the floor.

"Auntie Sue!" Emma squealed and hugged the woman

who had been holding the twins. "I didn't know you were coming!"

"When your mom said babysitting was available, I jumped at the chance," Emma's aunt said, and smiled. She looked a lot like Mrs. Kim. "I know the twins will be in good hands with you. And you've got plenty of help tonight!"

Jessi narrowed her eyes and muttered to me, "We're totally outnumbered now. Too bad Zoe and Frida couldn't make it."

The moms left us with diaper bags, snacks, and plenty of instructions.

"No juice for Sophia. Water only, please!"

"Mason can get a little rambunctious. It's best just to let him tire himself out."

"Lily didn't have a nap this afternoon. She's a little fussy."

Lily was the one who had been crying when the women had walked in. Her big brown eyes were red, and she hung on to her mom's leg.

"If you need anything, we'll be in the movie room," Mrs. Kim said.

The moms thanked us before leaving, and then we were left alone in the room with five toddlers. I had a little sister and had taken babysitting classes, but this was a lot to handle. This was turning out to be a big-sister boot camp for Jessi!

The twins were Emma's cousins, girls named Ava and

Emily. They wore cute matching purple striped leggings and T-shirts. Emma swore she could tell them apart, but I didn't think I'd be able to. They looked identical to me!

Mason immediately ran over to the cubbies and pulled out a book. Sophia, who had light red hair in pigtails, toddled over and tried to grab it from him. Mason hit her over the head with the book. Luckily, it was one of those soft, squishy ones, so I knew Sophia didn't get hurt. But that didn't stop her from screaming at the top of her lungs.

"Five seconds of babysitting, and it has already descended into chaos," Jessi complained, covering her ears. "This is what I have to look forward to?"

Emma scooped up Sophia. "Do you want to play blocks with Ava and Emily?"

Sophia stopped crying, and Emma grabbed a basket of blocks, sat down with the three girls, and started building with them. Mason was still rifling through the cubbies.

"Is he looking for something harder to hit Sophia with this time?" Jessi wondered.

Lily sat by the door. She hadn't moved since her mother had left. Her lower lip was quivering, and I thought she might burst into tears at any second.

"Do you want to take Mason and I'll take Lily?" I asked.

"I feel like we're on the soccer field, covering other players," Jessi joked. "Okay, Coach!"

Mason had gotten another book out. "Read!" he demanded as he handed it to Jessi. She sat down on the floor next to him, and he plopped into her lap.

Jessi began to read as I approached Lily. I sat on the floor next to her. "Hi, Lily," I said softly. "Do you want to play? We could play blocks with the other girls?" I pointed at Ava, Emily, and Sophia.

Lily sniffled. She pointed at the door. "Mama," she said.

"Mama will be back soon," I said. "Let's go play." I tried to pick her up, but she stiffened her entire body and started screaming.

"Noooooooooooo!" she cried.

Emma left the girls playing and came over to help.

"It's okay, Lily," she said soothingly. "Do you want me to read you a story?"

But Lily only cried more loudly.

Jessi looked up. "I guess I got the easy one," she said. Mason was very quiet, sitting in her lap. Then Jessi wrinkled her nose. "What's that smell?"

"Poopy!" Mason said triumphantly. He smiled. "I made poopy!"

"Ugh!" Jessi slid Mason off her lap as if he were radioactive. She stood up and hurried away from him. "I'm not changing that diaper. A baby is one thing, but that kid is eating solid foods, and a lot of them, I'm guessing from that smell. Not it!"

Lily kept crying and wouldn't move away from the door. "Mama!" she sobbed.

The smell of Mason's diaper drifted over to me too. "Uh-oh," I said to Emma. "That smells like a two-person job."

"At least Ava, Emily, and Sophia are playing nicely," Emma said as she glanced at the girls, who were engrossed in the colorful blocks. "Devin and I will change Mason's diaper. Jessi, can you try to calm Lily down? Nothing seems to be working."

"So these are going to be my choices in the future—disgusting diaper or nonstop crying?" Jessi asked with a roll of her eyes. "Whatever."

Emma got the diaper bag Mason's mom had left, and she and I got to work as Jessi sat with Lily, who kept on sobbing.

"Hey, don't cry," we heard Jessi say as we cleaned up Mason.

"Mama!" Lily continued to cry.

As I handed Emma some extra baby wipes (Jessi might have been right about Mason!), she frowned with concern.

"If Lily keeps crying like that, I'll get her mom," Emma said. "I don't think anything is going to make her happy."

We finished up with the diaper change, so engrossed in what we were doing that we didn't pay attention to anything else. Once Mason was clean and dry with a fresh diaper, we noticed something: The room was very quiet.

"Hey, Lily isn't crying anymore!" Emma said.

I laughed as I pointed. "That's why!"

Lily was sitting with a baby blanket over her head.

"Where did Lily go?" Jessi asked in a loud, wondering voice. "I can't find her anywhere!"

Lily grabbed the blanket off her head, her brown hair sticking up as she smiled broadly.

"There she is!" Jessi said. "I found her."

Then Lily got up and toddled over to Jessi, the blanket in her hand. She put it over Jessi's head.

"Where did Jessi go?" Jessi asked from under the blanket. "Lily, can you find me?"

Lily pulled the blanket off Jessi's head, laughing as she did.

"You did it!" Emma cried, clapping her hands together. "You got her to stop crying!"

Jessi shrugged. "It was no big deal."

"I couldn't do it," Emma reminded her. "And Devin couldn't do it either."

A grin broke out on Jessi's face. "Hey, you're right! Maybe I'll be able to get the hang of this big-sister thing, after all."

"The next diaper is all you," I told her.

Jessi put her hands up into the air, as if to block a barrage of dirty diapers flying at her.

"One thing at a time!" she laughed.

CHAPTER FOURTEEN

"Where are they? Where are they? I can't see anything!" Maisie complained next to me.

We were in the airport, waiting for Grandma and Grandpa to come out through the boarding gate. It was Sunday afternoon, and the place was really crowded. People kept bumping into us as they hurried through the terminal. And while we saw lots of people walking down the ramp toward us, none of them were Grandma and Grandpa.

"Be patient, Maisie," Mom said, gently putting a hand on her head. But I could tell that Mom was just as excited as Maisie. She jumped a little bit anytime somebody who looked like Grandma or Grandpa appeared.

Finally we saw one head of short, brown hair and one bald head appear over the wave of people getting off the plane. Then I heard a loud voice.

"Noodles! Maisie Daisy!"

"Grandma!" Maisie shrieked, and Mom had to hold her back from going through the gate. But Grandma and Grandpa hurried toward us, and soon I was wrapped in Grandma's peppermint hug, and Grandpa had picked up Maisie.

Then it was Mom's and Dad's turns to do the hugging.

"How was your flight?" Mom asked.

"Just lovely," Grandma said. "I finished my book."

"And I slept," Grandpa replied, putting Maisie down so he could stretch.

"So you're not too tired?" Dad asked. "We were thinking of taking you on a little tour of the town on the way home."

"Sounds good, as long as one stop on the tour includes some California cooking," Grandpa said. "That airplane lunch they gave us wasn't enough to fill up little Maisie here, let alone a grown man."

"We could go to Atomic Burrito," I suggested as we began walking through the terminal. "The burritos here are much better than they are in Connecticut."

"Oh dear, that sounds very spicy," Grandma said.

"Let's go to Pirate Pete's Pizza Palace!" Maisie suggested. "There's a talking parrot that's really a robot there!"

"Actually, I made us early dinner reservations at the Palm Café," Dad said.

I wiggled my eyebrows. "That place? It's fancy, isn't it?" I looked down at my flip-flops, which I wore almost all the time now, except when I was playing soccer or practicing soccer.

"We can sit on the patio. It's more casual out there," Mom said.

It took us a while to get the bags, but soon we were all piled in the Marshmallow and heading to Kentville. Dad drove past Maisie's school, and my school, and then the soccer practice field that the Kicks used.

"Is this where the magic happens, Devin?" Grandpa asked.

"Well, sometimes . . . ," I replied, and my voice trailed off.

"They lost the last two scrimmages!" Maisie piped up.

"Maisie!" Mom scolded.

"No, she's right," I said with a sigh. "Our season isn't getting off to such a great start."

"And it didn't help that Devin pulled a muscle," Dad added.

"Oh no! Are you all right, Noodles?" Grandma asked.

"It's all better now," I said. "I should definitely be ready to play in our first game on Saturday."

"I can't wait!" Grandma said. "If you have some craft supplies at the house, I'd love to make a sign to cheer you on."

"Thanks, Grandma," I said. "Just as long as it doesn't say 'Noodles' on it!"

We both laughed, but inside I was feeling worried. I could imagine Grandma and Grandpa in the stands, Kicks blue on their faces, cheering like crazy . . . while the Kicks went down in flames against the Panthers.

Then we pulled into the Palm Café parking lot, and

everyone forgot to talk about soccer. We sat on the patio in the bright California sunshine and ate salads with grilled chicken while Grandma and Grandpa talked about the family back home.

"Your cousin Jason is doing very well," Grandma told us. "He's on the school baseball team this year."

"I don't know how we ended up with such an athletic family," Grandpa said. "The only sport I'm good at is darts!"

"Why didn't you order the noodles, Noodles—oops, I mean Devin?" Grandma asked.

"Grandma! I don't even remember when all I would eat was noodles," I replied.

"I'll never forget. You were three years old. You ate buttered elbow macaroni, buttered spaghetti, buttered penne, buttered shells, buttered fettuccine. Any kind of buttered noodle, you would eat, and nothing else. Your mother was beside herself. You would point at your mouth and say 'noodles' whenever you were hungry." Grandma laughed. "It was the cutest thing. You loved it when I called you 'Noodles' because you loved eating them so much."

"I'm so glad her diet has improved," Mom said. "She eats a variety of healthy foods now, thank goodness."

"Hey, so do I!" Maisie complained, which was really funny, because we basically had to trick her into eating food that was good for her.

My phone vibrated, and I looked down to see a text from Frida.

Can I come over and borrow your English book? Left mine in my locker.

I had already finished my English homework, so I knew it wouldn't be a big deal.

"Mom, Frida needs to borrow my English book," I told her.

"Tell her to come by in an hour," Mom said. "We'll be home by then."

Come by at 6, I texted back. *You can meet my grandparents.*

☺ Frida replied.

I was kind of excited for Grandma and Grandpa to meet one of my new friends. They really didn't know much about my life in California.

We finished our meal and went back to the house. Maisie and I helped carry Grandma's and Grandpa's bags with us. They started oohing and aahing over everything.

"So bright and sunny in every room!" Grandma said.

"And those plants! I bet they grow all year round," Grandpa remarked.

They were settling into the guest room when the doorbell rang. I opened it to see Frida standing there.

"Devin, dahling," she said, and she kissed me on the left cheek, and then the right one.

"Wow, you're all dressed up," I said. Frida had her hair in that swept-to-the-side style again, and she was wearing a red dress with a flouncy skirt, and shiny black flats.

"Oh, this old thing?" she asked, flipping her auburn hair

with her hand. "People just don't dress up enough these days, that's what I think."

I suddenly realized that Frida was sounding more and more like Miriam, the film actress from the senior home. She'd had the new hairstyle the other day at Jessi's, but now she was really going all out. Normally she saved her characters for the soccer field, but it looked like Miriam was spilling over into Frida's real life more than ever.

Grandma and Grandpa came downstairs. "Noodles! Is this your friend?" Grandma asked.

I turned to Grandma and gave her my please-don't-call-me-"Noodles" look. But Frida was already walking toward them with her hand outstretched.

"Wonderful to meet you," she said. "I'm Devin's friend Frida."

Grandpa took Frida's hand and pumped it hard. "Nice to meet you, young lady."

"Are you on Devin's soccer team?" Grandma asked.

"Yes, but that is mostly for exercise," Frida replied. "I am an actor by trade."

"How nice for you," Grandma said. "I would imagine that there are a lot of opportunities for actors out here."

Frida flinched a little bit. "Yes, but it's a very difficult business at the moment."

"So is soccer," I pointed out.

"Well, we have had a rough start this season," Frida admitted. "But our team still looks very promising. We've got a new player, Hailey, who's simply fantastic."

I inadvertently flinched when I heard Hailey's name. It was bad enough that I hadn't been playing my best yet this season—but seeing Hailey succeed when I wasn't made it worse. Which stank, because I really did like Hailey!

"Let me go get that book," I said, taking two steps at a time up the stairs to get to my room.

When I came back down, Frida and my grandparents were in a deep conversation about some actress named Katharine Hepburn.

"You've got her hair, young lady," Grandpa was saying. "If you've got her talent, too, you'll go very far."

Frida was beaming. "Thank you!" Then she noticed me. "And thanks for the book, Devin. I'd better go. My mom's waiting in the car outside."

"That friend of yours is quite a character," Grandpa said after Frida had left, and I couldn't help smiling.

"Yeah, that's the exact right way to put it!"

The rest of the night with Grandpa and Grandma was nice and relaxed. Grandma played a board game with me and Maisie while Grandpa napped. Then Mom made us all a snack because we had eaten dinner early. When Maisie's bedtime rolled around at eight, Grandma and Grandpa announced that they were getting ready for bed too.

"There's something about planes that wipes the energy out of you," Grandma explained. She gave me a kiss on the forehead. "See you in the morning, Noodles."

As I made my way up the stairs to my room, I realized

my leg wasn't bothering me at all. In fact, it felt great.

One early-morning jog won't hurt, I told myself. *I'll take it easy. No parkour this time.*

But when I crept downstairs the next morning in my running gear, a delicious smell filled the air. The light in the kitchen was on, and I saw Grandma in there, wide awake.

"Devin!" she whispered. "Come eat breakfast with me."

I hesitated. Then I jogged into the kitchen. "I'm going on a run," I whispered back.

"A run? This early?" Grandma asked. "Can't you take a morning off and have a muffin with your grandma? I just baked them."

I spotted the muffins cooling on the counter. The smell of apples and cinnamon was too hard to resist. It smelled like Connecticut. I opened the fridge, poured myself a glass of milk, and sat down at the kitchen table. Grandma brought me a muffin still steaming and sat down next to me.

"Thanks for skipping your run," she said. "You're working awfully hard, Devin. I know soccer means a lot to you."

I nodded. "It means everything!"

"And I can tell that it bothers you that the team is having a rough start," Grandma said.

I bit into the soft, warm muffin, thinking. "Of course it bothers me," I answered. "I mean, I always want to win. But now everyone is expecting us to win. The school, the parents, even the town!"

Grandma gave me a sympathetic nod. "That sounds like a lot to handle."

"It is!" I cried, forgetting that everyone else was still sleeping.

"Just make sure you don't put too much of a burden on yourself, Noodles," Grandma said. "There will always be demands in life. There's nothing you can do about that. But you can be kind to yourself. Putting too much stress on yourself can lead to trouble—like a pulled muscle."

I must have blushed a little when she said that. Grandma knew me so well!

"You don't have to be better than anyone else, Devin," Grandma said. "Just do your best. Do what you know how to do. No pressure."

"No pressure," I said, but it was much easier to say than to actually feel.

Mom came into the kitchen, yawning. "I thought I heard voices. What are you two doing up so early?"

"I couldn't sleep," Grandma said. "And Devin was about to go for a run, but I talked her into a muffin instead."

Mom smiled. "Only you could do that, Mom," she said, hugging Grandma's shoulders. "I'm glad you're here."

"Me too," I said, and then I got up and grabbed another muffin. If I wasn't going on my extra run that morning, I thought I might as well have seconds.

Grandma's grandmother powers were beginning to work. I was starting to feel the heaviness lift, just a tiny little bit.

It felt good.

CHAPTER FIFTEEN

I gave up my early-morning runs over the next week and concentrated on practices. Believe me, they were tough enough. Coach Flores must have been feeling the heat too, because she had us drilling more than ever before.

We didn't have any scrimmages that week, which was kind of a relief. It gave us a chance to focus on making ourselves better, and not worrying about what the other teams were like.

When I got home from practice on Wednesday, Grandma was helping Maisie with her spelling words, and Grandpa was making his world-famous chili. (Well, he said it was world famous, but I don't know that for sure. It's definitely famous in our family, though.)

"How did practice go, Noo—I mean, Devin?" Grandma asked me, looking up from the kitchen table.

"Great!" I replied, and I realized it was true. The Kicks

had been a little rusty after the winter break, and I think it had taken us some time to find our rhythm again. But we were passing to each other much more smoothly and communicating better on the field.

Still, I had butterflies in my stomach about Saturday's game. Losing to Pinewood in the scrimmage had been rough, but it had been just a scrimmage. If we lost the first real game of the season, I knew we would be letting everybody down.

"Did you tell her the idea?" Grandpa asked, stirring the big pot of chili on the stove.

"What idea?" I asked.

"Well, Grandpa and I would like to throw a barbecue on Friday for you and your teammates, on the night before the big game," Grandma said. "Your mother told me that sometimes you all go out for pizza or frozen yogurt, so we thought it might be nice to host everyone here."

"Really? That would be so cool!" I said. In the fall I'd started organizing team get-togethers to help with team building. A pregame barbecue was a great idea.

Grandma smiled. "I thought you'd like it. Your mom is taking care of emailing your teammates' parents. Grandpa and I will take care of the food."

"I'm making extra chili so we can have chili dogs!" Grandpa announced.

I reached down and gave Grandma a hug. "You guys are the best! Thanks!"

I really did have awesome grandparents. When I got home

from school on Friday, I found the backyard decorated with white and blue balloons, and the tablecloths, paper plates, and napkins were all Kicks blue. Grandpa was cleaning the grill, and Grandma and Mom were in the kitchen, surrounded by what looked like every bowl we owned.

"What can I do to help?" I asked.

"Wash your hands, and then you can start filling some bowls with chips," Grandma said. She looked at the clock. "Your teammates should all be here in about an hour."

The hour went quickly. I filled up a big tub with ice and bottles of water and soda. When it got closer to party time, I helped Grandma carry out bowls and bowls of salad—sesame noodle salad, macaroni salad, potato salad, black bean salad, jiggly green gelatin salad, and regular salad. There were plates of pickles, and dip for the chips, and mountains of burgers, veggie burgers, and hot dogs ready for the grill, along with a small pot of Grandpa's chili. On the dessert table was a fruit salad and four of Grandma's Boston cream pies. They had a graham cracker crust, chocolate pudding for filling, and whipped cream on top. Yum!

Dad came home from work just as the barbecue started. It seemed like the whole team showed up at once: Jessi, Emma, Zoe, Frida, Brianna, Sarah, Anna, Olivia, Grace, Megan, Giselle, Gabriela, Anjali, Alandra, Taylor, Maya, Zarine, and Jade. Even Coach Flores came.

When Hailey came, she smiled at me and gave me a big hug. "Thanks for having us all over, Devin!"

I felt a pang of guilt. Hailey was so nice. And it had been

my idea for her to try out for the Kicks. I was still feeling jealous of her awesome skills. But we weren't at a soccer game or practice, so I decided to forget about it and focus on fun.

Everyone started talking right away, and grabbing plates of food. I brought my best friends over to meet my grandparents at the grill.

"Grandma and Grandpa, these are my friends Jessi, Zoe, and Emma," I said. "And you guys met Frida already."

Grandpa was busy flipping burgers, so Grandma shook everyone's hand.

"So nice to meet you," she said. Then she looked at me. "You have such lovely friends, Noodles!" Her hand flew to her mouth and she gasped. "I mean Devin."

But she had caught herself too late.

Emma started giggling, and Jessi's eyes got wide. "'Noodles'? Oh my gosh, that is perfect."

"Yeah, well, it's kind of a family thing," I explained, blushing.

Jessi grinned. "Whatever you say, Noodles!"

I knew I had to change the subject. "Come on, let's get some plates and eat!" I said.

We grabbed plates and then got what we wanted from the grill. (Veggie burger for me, hot dogs for Emma and Jessi, hamburgers for Zoe and Frida.) Then we went to the food table to get our salad.

"Is that noodle salad I see?" Jessi asked.

"Yes, it is. Sesame noodle salad," I replied calmly, ignoring her teasing.

"This looks like amazing noodle salad," she said, spooning some onto her plate. "Did you make this, Noodles?"

"No, my grandmother made it, and please do not call me Noodles," I replied.

I turned quickly and marched over to one of the tables and sat down. Zoe and Frida sat on the same side as me, and Jessi and Emma took seats across from us. I took a bite of my veggie burger.

"How is that veggie burger, Noodles?" Jessi asked.

I put down the burger. "Please. Do. Not. Call. Me. Noodles."

"Aw, come on," Jessi pleaded. "It's so much fun to say. Noodles! Noodles! Noodles!"

Emma was giggling again. "It is really cute, Devin."

Zoe nodded. "It definitely has a ring to it. Noodles Burke."

I groaned. "Oh, I knew this was going to happen!"

Jessi reached over and patted my arm. "It's okay, Noodles."

I picked up some of the sesame noodles from my plate. "These are noodles!" I said. I waved the noodles at Jessi. "I am not Noodles!"

As I waved my hand, the slippery noodles flew out of my fingers—and landed on Jessi's face. She started shaking her head.

"Oh, no you didn't!" she said.

I couldn't help giggling. "Jessi, it was an accident!"

Jessi picked up a forkful of green gelatin salad. She held up the fork and moved it back, like she was going to fling it at me.

"No!" I squealed, and ducked.

The jiggly green gelatin flew over my head and landed with a splat on Grace's neck.

"Gross!" she cried. Then she turned around. "Who did that?"

"It was Jessi! It was Jessi!" I cried, laughing.

Grace got a gleam in her eye. "Oh yeah?" She put some potato salad on her fork and stood up to face Jessi.

"It was an accident! I was trying to hit Devin!" Jessi protested, but Grace sent the potato salad soaring toward Jessi. Jessi moved fast, grabbing a fistful of noodle salad and hurling it at Grace.

"Mom! Dad! Devin and her friends are having a food fight!" I heard Maisie yell, and then I saw her run into the house to get them.

"Did somebody say food fight?" Anna called out. She jumped up and grabbed her paper plate.

I jumped up too. "No! Wait!" I called out, but a glob of macaroni salad was aiming for my forehead.

Then chaos erupted. My teammates started hurling food at each other! Noodles, tomatoes, grapes, potato salad, hot dog buns—you name it!

Grandma stepped into the middle of the fray. "Now, girls, I know that—" she started to say, but stopped when a piece of Boston cream pie hit her in the face.

Suddenly everyone stopped throwing food, and the yard got quiet. I held my breath.

Grandma wiped some of the whipped cream off her cheek and tasted it. "Delicious!" she said. "But much better in our stomachs than on our faces, don't you think?"

Everyone started laughing then, and I looked around. We were all a mess! Emma had a red tomato stain on her white tank top, and Zoe's face had a big splotch of chocolate pudding on it. Nobody had been spared.

Mom and Dad came out of the house, followed by Maisie.

"What on earth is going on here?" Mom asked.

"I think these girls needed to let off some steam," Grandma said. "And I can't say that I blame them. But they're going to clean everything up now."

We all nodded.

Then Grandma turned to Maisie. "Get the garden hose."

A grin came over Maisie's face. "You got it, Grandma!"

Dad sighed. "I'll get some beach towels."

After we cleaned the food off the lawn and the tables, we lined up, and Maisie hosed each of us down. She looked happier than when she was playing video games. We dried off with beach towels and then sat back down to finish eating.

"I got another round of hot dogs here. Chili dogs!" Grandpa said, and a bunch of girls got up and made a beeline for the grill. I walked up to Grandma.

"Sorry, Grandma," I said.

Grandma smiled. "It's okay. I made plenty of food," she said. "And let me tell you something—if you girls bring the same energy to your game tomorrow, you're going to win for sure!"

She said it loudly, and all the Kicks let out a cheer. I just hoped she was right!

CHAPTER SIXTEEN

Even though I knew the Kicks would have good fan turnout for the Pinewood game after the newspaper article, I still couldn't believe my eyes when I got to the field. The stands were a sea of blue and white, packed with our families and friends ready to cheer us to victory!

There was a lot of Pinewood purple too, but for an away game it was a pretty amazing showing for the Kentville Kangaroos.

I gulped as the butterflies in my stomach started waking up and stretching their wings. Letting off steam and having such a blast at the barbecue the day before had really calmed my nerves. But the sight of so many people got my anxiety kicked back up. What if the parents started yelling again? I didn't think I could handle that stress on top of everything else.

As if she could read my mind, my mom put her hand on my arm.

"The parents should behave themselves during this game," Mom said. "We had an informal meeting at your last practice and talked it out. Everyone agreed it was best to back off."

I smiled as I felt at least that one worry disappear. "Thanks, Mom!" I hugged her.

She squeezed me back before handing me a bottle of water. "Remember to keep hydrated!" she said.

I ran onto the field to warm up with the other Kicks. I reached up to touch my pink headband and make sure it was securely in place. If I had anything close to a lucky charm, the headband was it. I had been wearing it since elementary school, ever since I'd first started playing soccer with my best friend, Kara.

I watched as the Panthers warmed up on the field, dribbling through cones with speed and precision. I spotted Mirabelle's head, her glossy black hair pulled back in her usual game-day French braid.

Jessi, Frida, Emma, and Zoe came over next to me, and for a second we all stood silently watching our competition.

"Those Pinewood girls always look like Amazons to me," Zoe said, breaking the silence. She was the shortest of my friends, so I could understand why that made her nervous.

Frida laughed, a chuckle very reminiscent of Miriam's.

"You're in luck, then, darling," she said. "Because today the character I have chosen is that of Antiope, the Amazon queen. It was Miriam's first starring role."

"Good!" Jessi said. "We need all the power we can get.

Amazons were, like, really strong women warriors, right?"

Frida nodded. "The strongest."

"That'll come in handy," Emma said. "It's a lot better than being one of the Sunshine Puppies on the field!"

We all laughed as we joined the rest of the team. Coach Flores led us in warm-ups. And I made sure to pay extra attention to my legs while stretching. I didn't want to pull a muscle during the game!

"Sock swap!" Grace called, and we gathered in a circle to swap socks with the person on our left. We all did our silly toe wiggles and laughed as we did, but something seemed off.

"Is it just me, or did the laughter seem a little forced today?" I asked Jessi.

"I faked mine," Jessi admitted. "I'm feeling the anxiety big-time. Everyone is here watching!"

I exhaled slowly, trying to calm myself as I took my place on the field. Grace, Hailey, and I were starting as forwards. Frida, Sarah, Giselle, and Jade were our defensive line, and Jessi, Zoe, and Anna held the midfield.

I heard someone yelling "Devin" loudly. I looked up. Sitting with my dad, mom, and Maisie were Grandpa and Grandma. I saw Grandma holding up a sign, and for a second I was afraid it would say "Noodles" on it. But instead it said, in bright blue letters, GO, DEVIN! Whew!

The ref blew her whistle and the game began.

The Panthers quickly got control of the ball, and they tore down the field with it, but our midfield was ready.

Zoe was going in for a side tackle, poised to steal the ball, when a member of the Panthers' offense blatantly grabbed on to Zoe's jersey sleeve to stop her.

The ref's whistle blew, and the Panthers got a foul. The Kicks had a free kick, and Zoe sent the ball directly to Hailey, who was open.

But Hailey fumbled the ball, and it went skidding directly to the waiting feet of a Panthers defender, who passed it back down the field.

Seeing that made me realize that Hailey wasn't perfect. I had built her up in my head to be my biggest competition. But we were a team, and we won and lost together. Not one of us was perfect, including me. Did I think less of Hailey as a player because she'd made a mistake? No way. Then why would I think less of myself? Or any of the other Kicks, win or lose? I felt like a lightbulb had gotten switched on in my brain, but I didn't have time to dwell on it. The game was on!

The Panthers kept committing fouls, with aggressive behavior and going offsides. Nervous energy radiated all across the field, and it was clear that the Kicks weren't the only ones who were feeling it.

We were making silly, careless mistakes, but so was Pinewood. Neither team was making progress over the other, until Jessi got a hold of the ball and ran away with it down the field, right toward me.

"Devin!" she yelled as she launched the ball to me. I felt my excitement rise. I had a clear path to the goal.

Suddenly a dark shape came rushing at me. I didn't know what was happening, but the ball that was headed my way ended up in the mouth of the dark shape. It was a black Labrador retriever!

The dog had run onto the soccer field to chase the ball. The dog began nudging the ball with its nose. When the ball rolled away from it, the dog began happily chasing it, its tail wagging the entire time.

The whistle blew as the game stopped. Jessi came running down the field.

"Here, doggie!" she cried, but the dog ran away from her outstretched arms.

Soon everyone, both Kicks and Panthers, was chasing the dog around, trying to get it off the field. The dog thought it was a game, and ran from one player to the next. I don't know if dogs can smile, but this one looked like it was.

"Shadow! Come back here, boy!" I saw a man standing on the sidelines, holding a leash in his hand. There was a park next to the Panthers' field. I guess the man must have let his dog off leash, and when Shadow had seen all the fun happening on the soccer field, he'd bolted.

Even though I was frustrated to have been so close to a scoring opportunity only to lose it, I had to laugh.

"This is crazy!" Zoe giggled.

"Hound of Hades, I command you to desist!" Frida yelled in character as the Amazon queen. The dog bounded over to her, jumped up, and licked her face, before racing away again.

"He does not respect your authority," Jessi yelled to Frida, before she broke out into hysterical giggles.

Finally Coach Flores snuck up behind Shadow and scooped the dog up into her arms. It was a big dog, and Coach Flores wasn't a big person, so I was pretty impressed. The dog started licking Coach all over her face.

"Stop! That tickles!" Coach laughed as Shadow's owner rushed out to meet her. He clipped the leash onto Shadow's collar and helped Coach set him down on the field.

"I'm so sorry!" he apologized. "I shouldn't have taken him off the leash. I didn't know there was a soccer game today."

A quick break was called to give everyone a chance to get their heads back into the game and get a drink before play started again.

"That is the craziest thing I've ever seen at a soccer game," Emma remarked.

Jessi grinned. "We did end up with a Sunshine Puppy on the field today after all!" she joked.

Everyone chatted and giggled, and I felt like the strain we'd all been under had finally lifted. When we took our places back on the field, I felt a calm focus descend on our team.

When a Panthers midfielder had the ball, Anna swooped in and stole it, making a nice move around the Panthers defender who was blocking me, opening me up to receive her pass.

Anna sent the ball my way, and I buried it into the far post, zinging it right past the Panthers' goalie.

The crowd went wild. I had scored the first goal of the game!

Grace and Anna came running over to high-five me. It was 1–0.

It turned out that a dog running loose on the field was just what the Kicks needed to get rid of our nervous energy. And the Kicks scoring a goal was what did it for the Panthers.

After that, Mirabelle played like a fire had been lit under her. Our defenders couldn't control her. She dribbled her way through our defense and sent the ball flying high over Emma's head. It brushed the tips of her fingers before landing solidly in the net behind her. We were now tied.

I heard some voices raised in the stands, yelling. It was hard to hear on the field during a game. Usually Coach was shouting so that we could hear her directions, and Emma was calling out to us from the goal. When people in the stands started getting noisy, it became totally confusing to the players on the field. This sounded as though Megan's dad, who had the loudest voice of all the parents, was saying something. I couldn't make out what it was.

Again, I had other things to worry about. After Mirabelle's goal, our defenders tightened up, making things really tough for the Panthers' offense.

"You shall not pass. I, as the queen, command you!" Frida's voiced boomed across the field. The Panthers' offense exchanged confused looks with one another, while Mirabelle just rolled her eyes.

"Ignore that weirdo," she told her teammates, which made Frida angry.

"Ignore me at your peril, girl. With just one word from me, the entire Amazon tribe will rain flaming arrows upon your head," Frida yelled.

Just then the whistle blew. It was halftime. The flaming arrows would have to wait.

All of the Kicks gathered around Coach Flores. She was about to give us one of her inspiring halftime pep talks when Megan's dad walked up to us and interrupted.

"When are you going to put Megan in?" he asked angrily.

Everyone glanced at Megan, whose cheeks flushed bright red. Poor Megan. If my dad did something like that, I'd be so embarrassed.

My grandmother had left the stands and was standing behind him as we huddled around.

"I'm sorry, I don't think we've been introduced," she said politely to him. "I assume you are the coach?"

"Me? No," he said, surprised.

"Are you sure?" my grandmother asked sweetly. "Because the way you were yelling during the game, I thought you must be."

"My daughter is one of the players," he said defensively.

"I just want them to win. Is there anything wrong with that?"

Grandma shook her head. "Of course not. But you have to remember that these young people are trying their best. Soccer is hard, and it gets harder when everyone is yelling at them from the stands. Let your daughter and all of the other players have a chance to listen to their coach. It's the most important thing they can do to win the game. Now, why don't you come sit with us? I've got some muffins, and extra poster board if you want to make a sign for your daughter."

With that, Grandma led the bewildered man away and back into the stands. He didn't know what to say.

"Your grandma is awesome!" Jessi whispered to me, a look of admiration on her face. I was pretty impressed with how Grandma had handled the situation too.

Coach Flores smiled at us. "It is important to listen to your coach. And this is what I have to say. Keep doing what you're doing. You're playing your best. I'm so proud!"

We huddled up in a circle and put our hands on top of one another in the middle. "Go, Kicks!" we yelled.

At the start of the second half, we were like a well-oiled machine. Zoe fed a shot to Grace down the left wing. Grace sent it soaring toward the goal, giving the Kicks a 2–1 lead.

But anything could happen in soccer, and when it does, it happens quickly, so we were all on our toes.

Frida, Sarah, Giselle, and Anjali made it practically

impossible for the Panthers attackers to get through.

"Move!" Mirabelle yelled in irritation once, shoving Anjali to the ground, which resulted in a foul for the Panthers and a yellow card for Mirabelle.

The frustration sapped Mirabelle's focus, and she couldn't figure out a way to get through our defensive line. A few times a ball got loose, thanks to one of the other Panthers forwards, but Emma made the saves.

We had several more scoring opportunities on the Panthers, but weren't able to connect again. Their defense had tightened up, resulting in fewer successful shots at the goal.

The clock was running out, and it looked like we might be able to pull this one off.

"We got this! Stay focused!" Grace shouted encouragingly to the Kicks.

I itched to make another goal to solidify our lead, and I got my chance—thanks to Hailey!

Hailey had possession of the ball and was running down the right wing, when two Panthers charged her. Hailey remained cool and calm, faking left and then running with the ball to the right. It threw the defenders off her long enough to give her a chance to pass the ball.

"Hailey! I'm open!" I yelled. Hailey heard me, and so did a Panther, who came running to try to intercept the pass.

But I was faster. I guessed all that extra running had paid off after all! I zoomed around the defender and got to the ball first. I sent it flying into the back of the open corner of the goal.

Yes! The crowd started clapping and hollering. We were now 3–1. The whistle blew, and time was called. The Kicks had won!

The entire town hadn't watched us lose. We hadn't disappointed my grandparents, who had flown all the way across the country to see me play. Sally Lane wouldn't be taking back all of our new equipment, and we'd get that new sod for our field. A smile filled my face. Despite the intense pressure, we had done it!

All the Kicks swarmed out onto the field, hugging each other in happiness. Grace had a huge smile on her face too. I could see the relief. We had set the tone for the season, and it was a winning one!

Even more important, I thought as we lined up to slap hands with the Panthers, we were back together as the Kicks. Win or lose, this was where I belonged!

CHAPTER SEVENTEEN

"Spike the *V*.

"Dot the *I*.

"Curl the C.

"What do you get?

"Victory!

"Victory!"

The Kicks chanted the cheer together, standing in a big circle with our arms around one another, jumping up and down with our excitement. We were at Tina's Taco Shack, eating outdoors at picnic tables to celebrate our win.

We ended our cheer with, "Goooooo, Kicks!"

I was glad that Jessi had suggested eating here. We were too rowdy and loud to be indoors!

We sat down and began to devour our tacos. Everyone was really hungry after the game.

"This is good, but your grandpa's chili dogs are better,"

Emma said between bites. "I hope your grandparents come back to visit a lot!"

"Me too!" I said, my mouth stuffed with a spicy taco called the Hornet. "I really liked having them here. And I'll miss Grandma's muffins, and Grandpa's world-famous chili."

"Speaking of world famous, I got a part," Frida announced. She was no longer the Amazon queen. In fact, tired out from the game, she didn't seem like a Miriam clone either. She was back to being Frida.

"Yes!" Jessi pumped her fist into the air.

"I knew you wouldn't be out of work for long," Emma shared. "You are too talented!"

"What is it?" Zoe asked.

"It's a commercial," Frida said. "And it's all thanks to Miriam that I got the part. So that means it's thanks to Jessi, too!"

"What can I say? Every once in a while I have a good idea," Jessi joked.

"This one was genius," Frida said. "Not only did Miriam give me confidence, but the retro hairstyle I've been wearing, inspired by all those old movies, is what got me the part!"

"Really?" Zoe wondered. "What kind of commercial?"

"It's for a music streaming service," Frida said. "I get to play two parts—a retro girl listening to music on an old-time phonograph, and then a modern girl listening to music on her portable device. My 'do really sold me to the casting agent."

"That sounds so cool!" Zoe replied. "So that must mean you'll have two different outfits. What are your looks for each?"

Zoe and Frida got into a huge discussion about fashion, while the rest of us went over the game, play by play.

"That final goal was sweet, Devin," Jessi said admiringly.

"I couldn't have done it without Hailey," I admitted. "She broke around those defenders and fed the ball to me."

"Three cheers for Hailey!" Jessi jumped to her feet, and everyone began cheering.

Hailey, sitting at the end of our table, blushed.

"Devin and I had some great teamwork on the field," she said.

I smiled at her. "The way you faked out those defenders was skilled, Hailey. I got to hand it to you."

"Let's face it, all the Kicks are just plain awesome!" Jessi yelled, and everyone clapped and cheered again.

Grace stood up. "We gotta admit, we did make some mistakes at the beginning of the game. We were all feeling anxious. Until Shadow showed up to save the day. I say, three cheers for Shadow!"

"Shadow, Shadow, Shadow!" everyone started chanting. The other people eating at Tina's Taco Shack were looking at us like we were crazy, but none of us cared. We were all too happy about our win over the Panthers.

When I got home after our taco celebration, I was still riding high. Yes, the Kicks had practice again on Monday and the season had only just begun. But for now I wasn't going to worry about the next game. I was going to enjoy our victory and the time I had left with my grandparents. They were catching a flight home the next day.

"Noodles!" Grandma hugged me tight. "I'm so proud of you!"

"You did great, Devin," Grandpa said. "Two goals—now that was something to see!"

"Thanks!" I said. "Our team worked hard."

"How about that dog on the field?" Grandma wondered. "I've never seen anything like that!"

As they talked, I felt myself get a little teary. I would miss them so much. Everything they had done—Grandma's pep talk, helping my parents throw the barbecue, their support and laughter. There was nothing I wouldn't miss! My grandparents had been so encouraging. It gave me an idea.

"Maisie," I pulled my little sister aside. "Do you want to help me plan a surprise for Grandma and Grandpa?" I whispered into her ear.

Maisie nodded, her eyes getting wide as I outlined my plan. "I know it's last-minute, but we can do it!"

"I'll let Mom know," Maisie answered in a loud whisper as I ran off to take a shower and change. We had work to do!

While Grandma and Grandpa were packing up their stuff, Maisie and I made a banner of our own. We also blew up some balloons and found some streamers left over from Maisie's last birthday party, which we hung in the dining room.

Dad was making his special turkey burgers, and after helping with the decorations, Maisie made her Everything and the Kitchen Sink Salad. It was a struggle to get Maisie to eat healthfully, until my mom let her make the side salad for dinner one night.

She'd thrown in raisins and even some goldfish crackers. At first I hadn't even wanted to try it, but it had turned out to be pretty good.

"Grandpa might make the best chili in the world, but I make the best salad," Maisie boasted as she tossed ingredients together in a bowl. It was never the same salad twice, but no matter what was in it, Maisie ate every bite on her plate.

I knew that both my grandma and grandpa had a soft spot for chocolate, so I made one of the only recipes I knew—brownies. It was pretty easy. I just mixed all of the ingredients together in one bowl and then poured it into a baking pan.

We got everything set on the table, and then Mom called Grandma and Grandpa.

"Dinner's ready!" she said.

They came into the dining room, and Maisie and I both yelled, "Surprise!"

"Isn't this something?" Grandma said as she eyed the balloons and streamers. "And just look at that banner!"

We had written, WE'LL MISS YOU, GRANDMA AND GRANDPA! LOVE ALWAYS, NOODLES AND MAISE. Maisie had gotten really artistic with a picture of both of them, an airplane flying in the sky, and a picture of her own face with tears falling down her cheeks. Maisie had a little Frida in her—my sister could be just as dramatic as my friend! I had kept it a little simpler, adding only a border of hearts and flowers around the edges.

"You even signed it 'Noodles'!" Grandma sounded surprised. "I'm sorry, Devin. I know you're growing up, but you'll always be Noodles to me. At least in my heart. From now on I'm only calling you Devin."

At the moment, I wouldn't have minded if she called me Noodles!

"I made dinner!" Maisie said, tugging at Grandpa's sleeve. "Come and eat!"

I stifled an eye roll at that. She had made only the salad, but leave it to Maisie to take all the credit.

"I bet it's delicious," Grandpa said. "I can't wait to try it."

As our family sat around the table to eat, I realized how lucky I was. The pressure had lifted. My grandparents were proud of me. And the Kicks were off to a great start! Even better, I knew that even if we had lost, my family still would have been proud of me. Who could tell what the season held?

Surrounded by family and friends like this, I knew one thing for sure—no matter how bad the pressure got this season, I wouldn't have to deal with it alone!